SAFARI

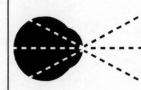

This Large Print Book carries the
Seal of Approval of N.A.V.H.

SAFARI

PARNELL HALL

THORNDIKE PRESS
A part of Gale, Cengage Learning

GALE
CENGAGE Learning·

Farmington Hills, Mich • San Francisco • New York • Waterville, Maine
Meriden, Conn • Mason, Ohio • Chicago

GALE
CENGAGE Learning®

LIBRARY OF CONGRESS CATALOGING-IN-PUBLICATION DATA

Hall, Parnell.
    Safari / by Parnell Hall. — Large print edition.
        pages cm. — (Thorndike Press large print mystery) (A Stanley Hastings mystery)
    ISBN 978-1-4104-7683-8 (hardcover) — ISBN 1-4104-7683-9 (hardcover)
    1. Hastings, Stanley (Fictitious character)—Fiction. 2. Private investigators—Fiction. 3. Safaris—Fiction. 4. Large type books. I. Title.
    PS3558.A37327S24 2015
    813'.54—dc23   2014049298

Published in 2015 by arrangement with Pegasus Books LLC

Printed in Mexico
1 2 3 4 5 6 7 19 18 17 16 15

For Jim and Franny

1
PACKING

"I don't want to go."

Uh oh.

That didn't compute.

Alice had been over the moon ever since a small inheritance from a great-uncle so obscure I wasn't sure who she was talking about — plus scrimping on a few non-essentials such as food and rent — had allowed us to fulfill her lifelong dream and book a cut-rate safari in Africa.

Since then she had been haunting Campmor, REI, EMS, Orvis, and countless other retailers I had never heard of before, and safari outfits, hats, boots, binoculars, sunscreen, insect repellent, and polyester underwear that dried so fast you could barely get them wet long enough to wash had been spread out in an ever-increasing array on the living room floor. Countless itineraries, checklists and maps poured from the computer. Flights had been booked, passports updated, and visas obtained.

Alice had talked about nothing else for months. So if Alice didn't want to go, something was terribly wrong.

There had to be an if.

"I don't want to go if you're not going to take it seriously."

Aha! So that was the problem. My lack of gravity. I wondered in what aspect of the journey I had failed in that department. From experience, I knew inquiring would not be wise. That would mean I had not taken the trip seriously enough to realize what she was talking about.

I had to be careful. I didn't want to say the wrong thing. "What do you want me to do?"

That was the wrong thing.

"*I* don't want you to do anything. *You're* the one who should want to do something."

I restrained myself from saying, "What should I want to do?" That would have thrown down the gauntlet and challenged Alice to a no-holds-barred dogfight where a win for me would be surviving with my marriage intact. "I want to go. I'm looking forward to it."

"Did you read the itinerary I printed out?"

"Of course I did."

"What do you think?"

"I think it looks good."

"Specifically."

"Ah —"

"What about bush camp?"

"Bush camp sounds good."

"You know what we do there?"

"We camp in the bush."

"If you're not going to take this seriously —"

"No, no. Wait a minute. That's where we go on game hikes."

"Uh huh. And what do we look for on a game hike?"

I almost said, "Game." Some guardian angel changed it to, "Wild animals."

"And what wild animal would you like to see most?"

"Tigers."

"Wrong continent. You might see a lion or a leopard."

"Great."

"How about the checklist I gave you?"

"I have it."

"Have you started packing?"

"Alice, we're not leaving until next month."

"We're leaving on the fourth. Have you gone over the checklist?"

"Of course."

"What have you checked off?"

"I haven't checked anything off. I just went over it to see what I need."

"What do you need?"

"Ah —"

"Stanley."

"I have a safari outfit."

"Actually, you have two. So you can change when one needs to be washed."

"Of course."

"Did you try on the harness?"

"Harness?"

I was not doing well. But with questions flying this fast I would be lucky to guess my name.

"For your binoculars. You need to practice putting it on."

I always thought binoculars hung from your neck, but that, Alice assured me, let them flop around and get in your way. She had found a harness that went on like a vest. The binoculars clipped into it. The harness kept them hanging securely above the waist, and still allowed them to be raised freely to your eyes.

"I can put on the harness," I said. I hoped I could. I was bluffing.

"I'll believe it when I see it. Do you know how to use the headlight?"

I stopped myself from saying, "Headlight?" I knew this one. The headlight was a tiny flashlight on a band you wore on your forehead to get around bush camp in the dark. "Yes, I do."

I expected her to make me prove it, but since I could, she didn't.

"You need to check off everything on your list, lay out anything else you want to take, pack your duffle, and weigh it. Some of our interior flights are on very small planes. Your duffle can't weigh more than fifteen kilos. Your carry-on can't weigh more than seven."

"What are we using for carry-ons?"

Alice looked pained. "Our backpacks, Stanley. We've been over this."

"Right, right. I'll get on it."

"Don't get on it, just do it. You need to pack now so you can see if there's anything else you need." Alice shook her head. "Seriously, Stanley. It's hard to cope with your lack of enthusiasm. Are you sure you want to go?"

"Are you kidding? I can't wait."

Then we could stop packing.

2
BUSINESS CLASS

Some days you get lucky.

Our flight was overbooked and they didn't have a seat for us. You probably don't think that's good news, but you're not married to Alice. My wife is not one to suffer long in silence. Her record can be measured in milliseconds. Alice had booked the seats. She had booked them correctly, and she had booked them well. If they were not available, heads were going to roll. Alice was either going to get satisfaction or wind up owning the airline.

The airline caved fast. The opening bid was five hundred dollars to take a later flight. That was not five hundred dollars cash, that was a five-hundred-dollar credit off any future flight, as if there was any chance Alice would ever fly with them again if she were bumped off this one. Within minutes Alice had that offer up to a thousand, which apparently was as far as lower-level lackeys were empowered to bid, any further compensation requiring management and/or lawyers.

It never got that far. Alice was pulled aside and told quietly, out of earshot of the other passengers, several of whom were also being bumped, that the problem had been solved. Alice and I were upgraded to business class.

Welcome to paradise.

I'd never flown business class before. I'd seen it sometimes, on those planes you entered and walked through business class to get to coach. And I had peeked through the curtains during the flight and seen the privileged few being served food and drink far superior to the slop being foisted on the unwashed masses. But that's the least of it.

There's the lounge. Before you even get on the plane, you are treated to the business-class lounge. I'd never been in one before, but I'd fantasized about them, much in the way schoolboys fantasize about the girls' bathrooms, imagining all kinds of wonders and delights denied the so-called stronger sex. (Or is that just me? If so, of course not, I never did that.) Only in this case it's true. The business-class lounge was all I'd ever dreamed of, and more.

I had envisioned a coffee pot, a soda dispenser, perhaps some beer and bar nuts.

Not quite. The dining wing featured a full-service buffet currently serving brunch, ranging from crepes to omelets to all varieties of muffins, scones, croissants, three kinds of bacon, two kinds of sausage, Nova Scotia lox, bagels, blueberry pancakes, strawberry waffles, and thick-cut French toast.

Alice left me to check out the food while she commandeered a nook of mini-couches where she could connect her iPad to the free Wi-Fi service. So I was standing there gawking at the opulent, far-too-rich-and-calorie-laden-to-meet-Alice's-approval buffet when a goddess caught my eye.

It was a young girl — and here I'm at a loss, for at my advancing age I can't really distinguish sixteen years old from thirty — but a fresh-faced girl in some tank-toppy thing or other, and a pair of faded jeans. She was toting a plate of French toast and surveying the omelets as if she could eat a dozen or so and look none the worse for wear. She leaned over, perhaps to compare the cheese omelet to the egg-white one, and I tried not to stare. It's hard at my age. Actually, it's hard at any age, but it's gotten worse lately. Not that I could see anything. We're not talking nipples here. All I could see was cleavage, but that's all you get

14

nowadays. Fifteen years ago women didn't wear bras. And when they did, they'd pretend they didn't. They'd hide them away. They'd tuck the straps carefully under the shirt as if the sight of a bra was embarrassing. Now they wear them as a fashion statement. I don't get it.

I knew I shouldn't look, but I'm a bad person, a dirty old man. The problem is I see myself as a teenager. I have to punch myself in the head and remember how old I am. I did, and moved away from temptation. By that, I mean the fattening food. The young lady was not temptation, just a flight of fancy.

I escaped to the relative safety of the coffee machine. I say relative safety because in the valley of the new and different, the clueless man is not king. The coffee machine had no controls whatsoever, just a picture of a cup of coffee nestled among fluffy clouds which could have passed for cappuccino foam. I would have liked cappuccino foam, but below the picture was merely an opening with a wire bottom typical for the setting of a coffee cup with spigots up top to dispense coffee. But there were no buttons to activate the spigots. I wondered what did. Prayer?

As I stood blinking at the machine in helpless confusion, I felt someone standing behind me. I turned around and there she was. Omelet girl. Little Miss Let-me-lean-over-and-let-you-get-a-better-look. I flushed with embarrassment, realized I looked embarrassed, and blushed some more.

She smiled. "Can't figure it out?"

Figure what out? How old she was? How old I was? How to get her to bend over again? I grinned like a goofy dope.

She pointed. "The coffee machine. You can't figure out how to work it."

I smiled. "Got me. There's no button to press."

"Touch the screen."

I touched the cup of coffee and the picture immediately became a menu.

"See?" she said. "The whole thing's a giant iPad."

"Of course," I said. "That's why I don't think of it. I'm too old for an iPad. It's not a mePad. It's a youPad."

She giggled. "You're funny."

I wanted to die. I didn't want to be funny. Not to a girl like that. To a girl like that, funny was a pejorative to a guy like me. Funny was what you called your old uncle Wally, the one who never married.

At that moment, the girl of my dreams was pushed aside by a she-dragon, an older malevolent version of the woman in question, obviously the mother. "What did I tell you?" she said meaningfully to her daughter, glaring at me with one eye.

I knew what she told her, and it had something to do with talking to strange men. I turned back to the coffee machine, touched the screen for a cappuccino. Realized I hadn't taken a cup. I grabbed one off the counter, slid it under the flow of coffee and steamed milk, barely missing any and hardly burning my hand. I took the filled cup and beat a hasty retreat back to the couches.

Alice was reading the *New York Times* on her iPad. There was a free copy of the *New York Times* right on our table, but I'm not one to argue with Alice.

"Pretty good cappuccino," I said.

Alice looked up. "It took you ten minutes to get coffee?"

"It's a confusing coffee machine."

I sat and sipped my coffee, resolved not to get into any more trouble before they called our flight.

Business class was on another level. Literally. The lounge was upstairs from the gate, but you didn't go back down to board the plane. You walked straight in from the lounge. Because the plane was a double-

17

decker, and the business-class seats were on top. As I walked down the ramp, I could see the two entry ramps down below. There were two of them because there were so many more economy seats. Not that the economy deck was any bigger, but the business class seats took up more space. They were not just roomy, they were roomy as in having your own room.

My seat was two seats wide. I was on the aisle, and the seat next to me was a window seat, only it wasn't, it was a little built-in table, with a book rack and a Wi-Fi screen.

I also had a TV screen mounted on the back wall of Alice's table, about three feet in front of me. Underneath the screen was a hollowed-out space under the table where I could stretch my legs.

Alice had the window seat, the mirror image of mine, though also facing front and a half seat ahead of me. The two seats were little cubicles. Alice and I were technically sitting together, but I couldn't see her, and she couldn't see me. I figured that was probably okay with her.

It worked for me too. I slapped on my headphones and immersed myself in a movie. The screen offered a zillion choices including Movies Still in Theaters, Movies Just Opening, Movies Not Yet Released, and probably some Movies Still in Principal Photography. I chose a mindless action movie of the type Alice wouldn't be caught dead at. Alice prefers movies with no gun-shots, car chases, special effects, or plot.

About an hour later I needed to go to the restroom, so I paused the TV and padded down the aisle.

The restrooms were in the back on the plane. So, I discovered, was the business-class bar. Drinks were free, so if you wanted you could hang out in the bar and get spectacularly stewed. I don't drink, but a Diet Coke seemed tempting. One of the restrooms was vacant, so I used it first.

When I emerged, Lolita was at the bar. Her back was to me, but it had to be her. No, it wasn't that I recognized her derriere, though it certainly looked good in those faded jeans. Not that I was looking.

I hesitated for a moment. Prudence said go back to your seat and watch the movie. But I wanted that Diet Coke. And it wasn't like I'd hit on her, despite what her mother might think.

I bellied up to the bar just as she got her drink. It looked alcoholic. I wondered if she was old enough to drink, or if in business class they just didn't care.

The bartender was an attractive woman,

young but not jailbait. She smiled, said, "What can I get you?"

"A Diet Coke."

The girl looked at me. "You're drinking soda?"

"They have very good Diet Coke on these flights. I ride business class just to get it."

She giggled. "But it doesn't have alcohol in it."

"What are you drinking?"

"A margarita."

"I know. You drink it just for the salt."

She giggled again. "That's right. I fly business class for the salt."

Uh oh. I was getting on far too well with the girl. That couldn't be good.

It wasn't.

"You been in the restroom yet?"

"Just now."

"Aren't they *amazing*?" She lowered her voice a little. "Wouldn't they be great for the mile high club?"

I smiled nervously.

"You a member?" she said.

"Can't say as I am."

"Wanna join?"

My heart skipped a beat. I was amazed it didn't stop. I smiled. "Couldn't afford the dues."

Behind me someone came up to the bar. I

prayed it wouldn't be Alice.

My prayers were answered. It was the lesser of two evils.

Mama barreled between us, turning her back toward me.

I took the hint, picked up my Diet Coke, and went back to my seat.

On my way out I heard Mama mutter, "There ought to be a law."

It occurred to me there was.

3
TOILET SEATS

We changed planes in Dubai, which was a bit of a letdown. The plane was older, smaller, and in poor repair. It also had empty seats, so we were unceremoniously bounced from business class. I didn't mind, but Alice was offended. She'd fought hard for the upgrade and figured it should apply all the way through. No doubt a host of conciliatory SkyMiles were in the offing.

At any rate, Alice and I suffered the ten-hour flight to Lusaka in coach. Actually, Alice suffered not at all, sleeping most of the way. I had the window seat, because Alice likes the aisle so she can get up and walk around and stretch her back and go to the bathroom without having to climb over me. She doesn't, of course; she goes right to sleep, and I have to climb over her. When I do, no matter how careful I am not to disturb her, she always stirs slightly and says "mumph," which freely translated means "this will be in the divorce complaint" and "guess who ain't gettin' nothin' on this trip."

I can't sleep on planes. I sit and watch movies, my attention span ranging anywhere from eighty percent to zero. Eighty percent is me wide awake and fully alert and missing things only by being what Alice likes to call dull and vague. Luckily, with Alice asleep there was not apt to be a quiz on the movie, so I watched with total assurance, if not total comprehension.

(I didn't see the girl, by the way. Not that I was looking, she wasn't there. Clearly she and mommy had purchased business class and were still there. Driving home the point, as if it were necessary, that a girl like that was out of my class.)

I also spent a lot of time winding my watch. I have the old fashioned windup kind — well, actually it's self-winding — what I mean is there's hands and numbers and you have to able to read it, a skill probably only a generation away from being extinct. Anyway, you don't have to wind it to keep it going. You have to wind the hands to set the clock. Dubai is nine time zones ahead of New York, so I had to wind the watch ahead nine hours. The watch doesn't wind well. The face looks at me as if to say, what the hell are you doing? The hands of time

23

ground slowly though exceedingly fine, and I managed to set the watch nine hours ahead on the flight to Dubai.

I had to set it two hours back on the flight to Lusaka.

Which blew my mind. The trip was long enough. Granted there was no direct flight from JFK to Lusaka, I understood we had to fly somewhere else first. Still, did we have to overshoot it by two whole time zones? The mind boggled.

Anyway, by the time we got to Lusaka, regardless of how many hours it took, it was daylight, and I had a wonderful view of the airport as we touched down. The terminal was long and flat-roofed. In front of it were a number of planes, all small single-engine prop planes, with the possible exception of a twin-engine or two, not significantly larger. We came to a stop in front of them and sat there on the runway, one huge 7-whatever-number-they-were-up-to-at-the-time-7 jumbo jet, a giant queen bee among drones.

I wondered if they had a ladder in the terminal long enough to let us exit. Not to worry. We walked down canopied stairs onto the runway.

Inside the terminal we were funneled through immigration. Our passports were not only stamped, but we were fingerprinted and had our eyeballs scanned. Apparently we passed, because we were waved on to collect our luggage. I had doubts whether business-class luggage downgraded to coach passing through umpty time zones and doubling back on itself would survive, but it did, and we lugged it to customs. Alice handed in the declaration sheet she had filled out on the plane stating we were tourists and had nothing to declare, and they waved us through. They never checked our duffles or backpacks. That was nice, but I couldn't help thinking of all the current prescription bottles Alice had insisted I get for every pill I brought, having read that Zambia was tough on drugs and you could get busted for a Sudafed.

We emerged from customs into the main terminal where an eager young man in a Clemson Safari cap held up a large sign on a stick which also read Clemson Safari. He was a skinny black man in safari shirt and shorts, clean-shaven, bright-eyed, with the whitest teeth outside a TV commercial. He had already snared four tourists and was looking around for fresh game.

"Clemson Safari?" Alice said.

The young man looked as if that were the most wonderful thing he had ever heard. I fully expected bells to ring, trumpets to blare, and a shower of confetti to rain down upon us as Alice was presented with a check for eighty million dollars. He consulted his clipboard and said, "Yes, yes! And you are?"

"Alice and Stanley Hastings."

It was too good to be true. She even got the bonus question right. He nodded enthusiastically and checked us off on his list.

We introduced ourselves to our fellow passengers. I missed their names, as is my fashion. There was a young married couple, no, not prepubescent, but younger than we were, and two women of indeterminate age but determinate size. The size was large. They were not obese, just solid, chunky. I could see them wrestling lions to the ground. I hoped it wouldn't come to that. The women had their luggage on an airport cart, the type of SmartCart that costs five bucks at LaGuardia or JFK.

I risked exposing myself as a total idiot and incurring Alice's wrath by inquiring, "What do we do now?"

He smiled. I think I could have asked him any question and he would have smiled. *Is it true you raped and murdered your mother?* "We wait for plane."

"Another plane?" I blurted. I couldn't help myself. We'd been in the air for twenty-four hours.

"Stanley," Alice said. "You know the itinerary. Weren't you paying attention? He doesn't pay attention."

The smaller of the two large women said, "He's just not happy. How long have you been traveling?"

"Don't ask me," I said. "I've set my watch in so many directions I'm not sure if it's Thursday or Friday."

"It's Saturday."

"See?"

The larger of the two women said, "Where did you come from?"

"New York City."

"Then you have an excuse. We spent two days in Amsterdam."

"We could have gone through Amsterdam," Alice said, "but the layover in the airport was too long."

And there they were, happy as clams, chatting away. While for me the bone of contention, what are we doing in this damn airport — partially answered with the threat of another plane in the offing — was still up in the air, so to speak.

Luckily the married couple jumped in. At least the wife did. She looked younger than her husband, or perhaps it was just the ponytail in which she wore her straw-

colored hair. But there was a spunky fresh-
ness about her, even in her loose green
safari outfit. Her husband, a rather nerdy
type, had that world-weary look of having
been beaten into submission.

"When is the plane?" the wife said. "We
don't want to miss it."

The young man smiled. "You will not. It
is our plane."

"When do we board?" I asked.

"We wait for two more guests."

I glanced around the terminal, saw what I
was looking for. "Then I'm going to the
men's room," I said.

That roused Alice from her conversation
with the Amsterdam women. "Are we about
to board? Stanley always goes to the bathroom when we're about to board."

I escaped to the men's room with as much
dignity as I could muster. I must admit, I
carried a bit of ugly American prejudice
with me, wondering what sort of facilities I
would find.

Surprise. Instead of being out in the open,
the toilets were in stalls, with doors, no less.
I picked the closest one and went in. Discovered it had no toilet seat, just the bare
porcelain bowl. I went out, picked another.
It also had no toilet seat. This did not bode
well. Neither of the other toilets had seats

either. It would appear there was either a serial toilet seat thief, or Zambia was taking extreme measures to combat the spread of sexually transmitted disease. Assuming no one sat on the bowl. Which was a pretty good assumption. All but the most obese would fall right in.

Unfortunately, I had to use the toilet. I will not describe the scene that followed, but if cleanliness is next to godliness, I was not godly.

I emerged from the stall, washed my hands quite well, and rejoined our little group.

The last two members had just shown up.

Lolita and her mother.

4
WELCOME TO THE JUNGLE

We flew in two planes. There were two, because we were eight, and the planes held five at best, and then only if the fifth passenger sat in the copilot's seat.

Lolita did not fly with us. The two married couples flew in one plane, the four women in the other.

The seats were cozy. Two them faced backwards. Alice pled airsick ess and faced front. I volunteered to fly backwards, but the other two stepped up and took those seats. I missed their names, but learned they were an American couple living in Paris. He was in international banking, and she did something for an artist. Nude model sprang to mind, but that's just me.

Our pilot was a young white man who didn't look old enough to vote, but who claimed he'd been flying for years, prompting visions of him sitting on Daddy's lap.

Alice was nervous enough that she managed to avoid mentioning I was a private eye. I'm never comfortable telling people that. Their perceptions come from books and TV, which couldn't be further from the truth. I chase ambulances for a negligence lawyer, a semi-permanent job to supplement my writing and acting gigs, which as I grow older are fewer and farther between.

We flew for an hour and a half and set down in the middle of nowhere. The airport consisted of a dirt runway, period. No terminal, no tower, no structure of any kind. Just a clearing in the trees long enough to land.

"Welcome to the jungle," I said.

The nebbishy other husband said pedantically, "Actually, a jungle is a rainforest. Zambia is relatively dry."

I'm sure Alice would have decimated him had she not been fighting airsickness. Or beat him out at decimating me.

There were two jeeps at the end of the runway, not on the runway, of course, but parked alongside. Each jeep was manned by a guide and a driver. Or a guide who drove, and an assistant. I figured we'd sort all that out later. At any rate, the four men descended on us with welcoming smiles. They retrieved our luggage and stuffed it in the back of one of the jeeps. They'd just gotten it put away when the other plane arrived. I got out the video camera and filmed it coming in.

Our pilot was younger. Bad as I am at estimating age, I say that without hesitation. The other pilot might have flown in World War II. A little old man with snow-white hair, he appeared to have trouble climbing out of the cockpit. The guides greeted him no less enthusiastically, as they did the passengers. The fact that they paid no special attention to Lolita I attribute to extraordinary discipline. Either that or all four were gay.

The guides stowed their luggage and helped us up into the jeeps, which had three tiered passenger seats, making each successive row a slightly harder climb. Once again the couples got in one jeep and the women in the other. I wondered if we'd maintain the same positions for the duration. I kind of hoped so. It would be uncomfortable talking to Lolita in front of Alice. Neither was likely to hold her tongue.

I looked back as we drove off. Our young pilot was already taxiing down the runway. The other pilot was still trying to climb into his plane.

It was hard not to identify with him.

We bounced out of the clearing on what

was either a road or a recent set of tire tracks. I was immediately disappointed. No elephants. No zebras. No giraffes. Just antelopes. They were not just antelopes, of course, they were impalas, or gazelles, or some such like, and our guide pointed each species out gleefully as if it were a marvelous find. Alice took it all in, and would doubtless have great fun at my expense each time I misidentified one. Anyway, there must have been a zillion antelopes.

Most likely that was because no lions were eating them.

5
ELEPHANTS IN CAMP

We arrived at camp, where every Zambian citizen who could muster a smile was assembled in the parking lot. I climbed down from the jeep, which was a fair distance even from the second tier. Alice handed me the camera before climbing down herself. I did not know how much that simple act of holding the camera bag would foreshadow my prime directive for the trip.

I helped Alice down and turned to meet the welcoming committee. First up was a skinny black man with a tray of wet facecloths. I accepted one and discovered just how dusty it was riding in a jeep with no windshield and no top.

A young black woman with a tray of tall drinks of some kind smiled and pressed one on me.

Alice pointed to it. "That's not alcoholic, is it?"

"He doesn't drink alcohol," a voice behind

me said.

Sure enough, Lolita came bouncing up, still rubbing her face with her washcloth. There was something sensual in the way she was doing it. I know that sounds stupid. You had to be there.

Alice was, and I'm sure she picked up on it.

I was saved from embarrassment by a large man booming in a hearty voice, "There they are! Welcome, welcome! I'm Clemson." He smiled smugly. "Yes, that's Clemson as in Clemson Safari. Hey, who was I going to name it after?" He chuckled at his joke. "Anyway, don't let that fool you. I'm just one of the gang."

Clemson was just one of the gang in a plus-size safari outfit that was bursting at the seams. It was as if the man were attempting to become one with his company by devouring the camp. For all that, he wasn't pudgy, just solid.

"Well, well, let's not hold them hostage in the parking lot," he bubbled, and ushered us in the gate.

"Oh, my god!"

Alice was right. "Oh, my god" described it. The camp was like an upscale lodge. Yes, there were tents, but there are tents and there are tents. The tent to our right was a lounge and bar, complete with comfortable couches, cushioned chairs, and expensive-looking coffee tables.

The tent to our left was a dining room such as might have catered a wedding in the courtyard of an East Hampton mansion. In front of us, a marbled terrace overlooked the most idyllic river ever.

But all that escaped our notice.

To the left and right of the terrace, on the grassy lawns between the tents and the river, were three elephants. The two together were a mother and a baby, the little elephant almost puppy-like in a clumsy, floppy way. The other was a large male or female, I couldn't tell at first glance.

Before I got a second, Alice was suddenly transformed into a wild person. "Stanley! Camera! Camera! Camera!"

She was so vehement, it took me a moment to react, the idiot-husband reaction time famed in song and story. I swung the backpack off my arm, zipped it open, pulled out the camera with the long lens. Alice grabbed it, whipped off the lens cap, focused on the baby elephant.

Alice was not alone. Half the members of our group were clicking a mile a minute, taking whatever type of picture cameras take now, I'm not up on this digital stuff. All I know is there's no film, there's memory, because Alice bought some for the trip. I know because she said witheringly she wished she could buy some for me.

Lolita was shooting movies. I had a video camera, an ancient implement in dubious repair, left over from the days when our son Tommie was a boy. And I knew I should get it and shoot the baby elephant. Alice would be displeased if I didn't. But if I did, would she think I was shooting video because Lolita was? I could just hear her ribbing me about that. And then there was the camera itself, embarrassingly old and outmoded. I didn't want to whip it out in front of Lolita. Yes, I know how bad that sounds. That's sort of what I was thinking.

Anyway, I opted out of going to the videotape, and observed my fellow tourists.

The only ones who weren't shooting pictures were two men and a woman who had been sitting on the couch in the bar but had gotten up to join the group. One of the men wasn't tall, but looked athletic, in a rugged, pretty-boy way. His safari outfit was short-sleeved with short pants. His safari hat hung down his back, probably to show off his full head of wavy brown hair. His smile was cocky, arrogant.

The other man, in contrast, was taller,

thinner, and probably older, though it was hard to tell as he wore aviator shades and a wide-brimmed safari hat pulled down over his forehead. His safari outfit was long-sleeved with long pants. His grin was non-existent.

The woman, also in a safari outfit, seemed amiable, and looked older than most of the people in our group. I hoped that included me.

I figured the three of them had been here for a while, and the sight of up-close elephants was not unusual enough to warrant getting out a camera.

The rest of us shot like crazy.

Clemson watched it all like a proud papa, as if he had carefully engineered our greeting. *"I want you two elephants down here on the left, you over here on the right. And I want you on your best behavior. No running off, and no charging the guests. And no pooping. Not right away. I want you to look cute first. Then when you poop they'll think it's even cuter."*

No such comment was forthcoming. Instead, when the clicking had died down, Clemson smiled, raised his finger, and said, "Now, these are not the only three elephants in camp. There are many many more, and they are not tame elephants. They do not live in camp, camp just happens to be in

38

the area in which they live."

"That's adorable," one of the two women said. The larger of the two. I still hadn't sorted out their names.

Clemson's smile was indulgent. "Yes. Adorable. They are also dangerous. Do you know where an elephant sleeps?" Before anyone could jump in, he said the punch line himself. "Anywhere it wants to. In the daytime you can walk around camp, but if an elephant is between you and the dining hall, you don't *go* to the dining hall. You wait for the elephant to leave, or for someone to come and help you. At night you don't go at all. After dark you can't walk around by yourself. Someone will come to your tent and get you for dinner. After dinner someone will take you back. There are no exceptions. At night you walk with a guide with a flashlight and a rifle."

"Rifle?" Lolita said. "You don't shoot the elephants, do you?"

"Of course not. That's just a precaution. The guns are rarely needed. And then only to fire a warning shot."

"You've never shot an elephant?"

"I've never shot an elephant."

"I mean the guides."

"I've never shot a guide."

Lolita giggled. "No, seriously."

39

Clemson, backed into a corner, took a breath. "No one wants to shoot an elephant. But we're not going to let an elephant hurt a guest."

"Has that ever happened?"

"Every camp has horror stories. The guides usually tell them on the last night when you're leaving."

"We're only here one night," Lolita persisted.

"You won't have any trouble. Just do what the guides say and you'll be fine."

The cocky young man who'd been sitting in the bar said, "It's not a problem. We got here yesterday. Nothing's scary. Everything's perfectly safe."

It was the wrong thing to say. I could tell Lolita would have preferred scary.

I could also tell she was eying the young man with more than a casual interest. Mommy, no doubt wanting to spoil the moment, stepped between them and said, "Are those elephants?"

We all looked where she was pointing. The tops of rounded forms could be seen poking out of the water in the middle of the river.

Bad luck for Mommy. Her question merely gave the young man a chance to show off as an old hand who'd been there a

40

whole day. "No. Those are hippos."

Lolita was delighted. "Hippos! How exciting!"

"Yes," Clemson said. "And one reason you can't swim in the river."

"You can't?" Lolita said. She sounded crushed.

I was unable to keep images of her in a bikini out of my mind.

" 'Fraid not. Hippos have big mouths. I don't mean they talk a lot. I mean they're huge. Wait'll you see 'em up close. Not too close, of course. But out of the water."

"They come out of the water?"

"Particularly at night. They come out to hunt for food. But you see them during the daytime too. When you do, leave them alone. For an animal that size they're remarkably fast. And they're very dangerous. What I said about elephants goes double for hippos. In fact, if you find yourself trapped between an elephant and a hippo, walk toward the elephant."

Lolita was listening bright-eyed to this explanation, but Mommy wasn't enjoying it. "You said that was one reason not to swim in the river. What's the other?"

Clemson's smile was smug. "Crocodiles."

6
PICTURES

They took us to our tent, which resembled a tent about as much as the Waldorf resembled a Motel 6. It had a canvas top and sides, but the front, facing the river, had doors and windows and a view to die for. In Manhattan it could have brought in twenty-two hundred a month as a studio apartment, even if the windows faced a brick wall. There was a bedroom with a king-size bed, and an antechamber leading to a bathroom which had an indoor shower and an outdoor shower. The showers, of course, faced the river, offering a spectacular view as you luxuriated in the hot and cold running water. Or sat on the flush toilet, complete with actual seat, no amenity too extravagant for the guests.

In the bedroom were cubbies, shelves, and hangers. It seemed silly to unpack since we were only staying for one night. Still, after two days of travel it would be nice to have new clothes.

"Wanna take a shower?" I said.

"You go first."

"I was thinking we could save on water."

"Ha ha."

"It wasn't a joke. I'm very conservation-minded."

Alice waved it away. "Yeah, yeah. I gotta download my pictures."

She whipped out her iPad, another one of those contraptions that makes me feel like a dinosaur. I can't afford an iPad. Alice couldn't either, if we weren't doing the trip splurge, of which the camera and the iPad and the safari clothing were all included, sort of like, if we're going to be evicted from our apartment anyway, we might as well have something to take with us. Anyway, Alice hooked up some sort of cable that magically transferred the pictures she had just taken to the iPad for viewing. I still shoot film for my job and have to drop it off for developing and pick it up the next day, so I find such instantaneous, non-celluloid photography a cheat, like if I can't hold it in my hand, it's not a picture.

I was careful not to express this view to Alice. Instead, with the promise of hot water, I ripped off my stinky, two-day-old traveling clothes and treated myself to a shower. I chose the indoor shower because it was closest and most convenient, not because I was convinced that if I was standing naked in the outdoor shower a herd of elephants and hippos would stampede in and maul me.

I got out of the shower, toweled off, and paraded around naked for a while. Not only did this fail to impress Alice, she didn't even notice. Ordinarily, a put-your-pants-on-you're-standing-in-the-window would have been forthcoming. The fact that it didn't showed how wrapped up Alice was in her photography.

A lizard the size of a pit bull slithered across the porch.

"Look at that!" I said.

"I've seen it before, Stanley," Alice said.

I sighed and began pulling clothing out of my duffle. I put on a pair of the synthetic jockey shorts that dried faster than cotton. I didn't like 'em. I like cotton. I'd worn a pair of cotton shorts on the plane, and had another pair for the return trip. I decided, screw it, somewhere between now and then I'd manage to wash the damn things. I pulled off the nylon underwear, pulled on cotton ones, and felt immediately better.

I put on a new safari outfit, which looked remarkably like the outfit I'd just taken off, aside from being clean. It consisted of a long-sleeved shirt, so as not to be eaten by bugs, but with sleeves that unbuttoned and rolled up, so as not to be too hot when bugs weren't biting; and safari pants, the legs of which zipped off, converting them into shorts for the same purpose. I snapped on my non-metallic belt, the cloth one with the plastic buckle, and was completely dressed.

Except for the shoes. I had Tivas and boots. Boots for hiking, Tivas for wading. I had another pair of sneakers for casual wear, but the twenty-four-inch duffle wouldn't hold everything, and they were one of the casualties. I only had the boots because I'd worn them on the plane. I put them on, laced them up.

I had a floppy safari hat to protect me from the sun. I put it on, went outside, and met an elephant.

I had nothing to protect me from the elephant. Obviously an oversight in packing.

There he was, large as life. Larger, actually. If you've never met an elephant, outside of a zoo, I mean, trust me, they're large. I went out on the porch, came around the corner of the tent, and there he was, lumbering along from the direction of the path I was about to take. Apparently it was his path, or at least *he* thought it was.

Pardon me, I'm being an inadvertent sexist, as so often happens to me in the course of my existence. I was referring to the elephant as he, and I must tell you that at that moment I had no idea as to its gender. Its genitals were the last thing in the world I was interested in at that moment.

I froze, backed around the corner, and beat a hasty retreat into the tent.

"Alice!" I said.

Alice, intent on her pictures, waved me away.

"There's an elephant!"

"Where?"

"Outside our tent!"

As if on cue, the elephant cleared the corner and lurched into view.

Alice, catching the movement, looked up from her iPad. Her eyes widened. "Oh, my god!"

Suddenly, she was all action, ripping cables out of the iPad and reprogramming the camera from download to shoot, or however the hell the damn things work.

The elephant, meanwhile, was not waiting for his close-up, he was meandering down the hill toward the river. This time I'm using the word "he" advisedly. The elephant was indeed male. In fact, he was hung like an elephant.

"Why didn't you tell me?" Alice said, which was par for the course, at once assigning blame instead of credit. She wrenched open the door, slipped out onto the porch, her camera clicking furiously.

The elephant took no notice, just continued lumbering toward the river.

"Wanna follow him?" I said.

Alice paused in her snapping to stare at me in disbelief. "Follow him? Did you hear anything the guide said? You don't *follow* elephants. You *stay away from* elephants. That's obviously their path down to the river. Do you want to be on it? I don't think so. Another elephant will come around the corner on its way to the river and where will you be?"

I pointed. "Right down there."

"Don't be an idiot. Look. He's going in."

The elephant was indeed going into the river. He waded in while the water got deeper and deeper until only the top of his back and head could be seen. All in all, he didn't look much different from the hippos in the river. I wondered if an elephant and a hippo would fight. I'd never heard of such a thing, but then my ignorance is boundless.

As the elephant swam off, Alice triumphantly went back into the tent to download her pictures.

I stayed on the porch, watched the river. Wondered if I should have another go at the path. What would I encounter? Probably nothing. I'd go out, the path would be clear, I'd walk to the lounge, help myself to a Diet Coke from the self-service bar Clemson had pointed out.

I figured I'd do better to rack up some quality husband points by taking an interest in Alice's photography. Particularly as she had yet to ask me how Lolita knew I didn't drink. It was something she was not likely to forget, and, as I explained, it would be good to have her on my side.

So I went back in the tent, not, you understand, for fear of running into another elephant, but merely due to the prudence of a loving husband. Alice had already connected camera and iPad and was perusing her latest pix. Her finger flicked across the screen, revealing picture after picture.

"My god," I said, "how many did you take?"

She gave me one of her you-don't-get-it looks. "Stanley. It's not a question of how many I *take*, it's a question of how many I *keep*. Most of them I can dump right away."

"Why?"

"Because they're no good. See? This one's

48

out of focus." She deleted it, flicked to another. "This one's fine."

I looked. This picture of the elephant walking down the bank toward the river looked identical to the one she'd just deleted.

"It looks the same."

"That's because you don't know how to look. This one's sharp. Crisp. It's just fine. The other one, if I enlarge it, it'll get fuzzy." She looked at the picture, frowned. "But the composition's not good." Flick of the finger. "This one's good. Now if he'd just turn his head."

"That's the trouble with elephants these days. Just don't know how to pose." It was an injudicious comment, liable to lose me all husband points.

Alice ignored me, kept flicking. The faster she went, the more her pictures resembled a kinescope movie of an elephant walking into the river.

"Well," Alice said. "Some of these may be all right if I color-correct them."

"You can do that?"

Alice smiled condescendingly, patted me on the cheek. "Of course."

I knew for a fact that Alice's expertise in photography came from a few video tutorials on YouTube. Granted it was more than I knew, still it seemed a dubious achievement to feel smug about.

Alice put down the iPad. "Guess I'll take a shower."

"Good idea."

"You *took* a shower."

"I thought you didn't notice."

"How could I not notice? You were waving your phallic symbol in my face."

"Speaking of which."

"Leave me alone. I'm taking a shower."

"Can I look at the pictures?"

"Sure."

"How?"

"Just slide your finger over them."

"But you're on the last one."

"Gee. Guess you'll have to slide your finger in the other direction. Think you can handle that?"

Alice went in the bathroom. Moments later I heard water running.

I was tempted to surprise her in the shower. Considered the consequences. The scenario did not end well for me. I rejected the idea. Sat down to look at the pictures.

It was kind of cool, scrolling with my finger. It sure beat the old-fashioned way. You took a picture, there it was. You knew immediately if you got it. No rude surprises a day later when you picked up the film.

Going backwards, I saw the whole sequence in reverse. There was the elephant swimming in the water. Graceful for a large, clumsy animal in reverse. And there he was climbing up the bank. And —

What the hell!

I scrolled forwards and backwards a few frames, just to make sure.

And there, behind the trees, up close to the bank, right where Alice had ridiculed me for wanting to go, told me it wasn't safe and only a moron would do it, was a flash of color from a brightly colored fabric.

There was no need to ask who that was.

Everyone in camp was wearing safari gear of drab khaki or green.

Except Lolita.

7
MARKING TERRITORY

At three-thirty we assembled in the lounge for tea. I liked their version of tea, which featured a wide variety of rich pastries as well as iced coffee, a huge pitcher of it already blended with milk and sugar, kind of like the prefab Frappuccinos Starbucks sells tiny bottles of for exorbitant sums, the type of luxury I indulge myself in every now and then if not saving every penny to go to Africa.

I helped myself to a glass of iced coffee and a slice of cheesecake. I have a weakness for cheesecake.

"Going to pig out?" Alice said.

I hate it when she does that, particularly in front of people. It puts me in the position of denying myself something I really want and looking pussywhipped, or asserting my independence by eating more than I intended. Today she did it in front of Clemson, who was not likely to be sympathetic to her point of view, large as he was.

"I was thinking of nibbling a saltine, but I don't see any."

"Got you there," Clemson said. "You gotta remember, there are no calories on safari. You can count 'em when you get home."

None of my fellow travelers seemed to be counting calories. A piece of cheesecake was pretty tame compared to some of the other plates. One woman had a macaroon, a piece of key lime pie, and cannoli. The husband of the other couple was eating chocolate mousse with whipped cream, which had to be worse than cheesecake, or there was no justice in the world.

Lolita was nibbling on a chocolate chip cookie. I wondered if that was her usual behavior, watching her girlish figure. She seemed more a devil-take-the-consequences girl.

I'd intended to check her outfit, to see if it really did match the fabric I'd seen in the pictures, but she'd changed into safari gear like everyone else. I couldn't help thinking she looked good in it. Or of her in the shower before she put it on.

I don't know about other men, but I wasn't enjoying my midlife crisis much.

The last two stragglers drifted in. They

were the two men who had arrived the day before. The one who'd taken a shine to Lolita gave her a nod and a smile on his way to the coffee pitcher. He poured a glass, cut off a piece of coffee cake. The one in the aviator shades and safari hat didn't appear hungry. He flopped down on the couch with a glass of unsweetened iced tea.

"So," Clemson said, taking charge. "Here's the plan for this afternoon. We'll set out at four and have sundowners in the bush. The guides will find a nice spot where we can stop, get out of the jeeps, have drinks, and watch the sun go down."

"What time does the sun set?" I said.

Alice rolled her eyes. I didn't know why. I mean, can't I ask a simple question?

The know-it-all kid said, "You're near the equator. The sun always rises and sets at six."

It was all I could do to stop from blurting out, "Is that true?" From Alice's reaction, it had to be.

"Of course," I said.

"That's right," Clemson said. "And we'll be having drinks then. Tell your guide if there's anything in particular you want. Beer, wine, soda. You can have a mixed drink, if you ask in advance. As long as it's on the rocks, not something blended or shaken."

Clemson held his hands and smiled. "Normally we would come back after sundowners for dinner. But since you're only here one night, we've scheduled a night drive."

"What's that?" the other husband said. There weren't a lot of husbands on this trip. I wondered if I was an endangered species.

"Just what it sounds like. We'll have a spotlight, we'll drive around and look for game. Is there anything anyone particularly wants to see?"

"I have a fondness for cats," I said.

Clemson smiled. "Everyone has a fondness for cats. If we're lucky, we might see a leopard. Don't count on it, but keep your fingers crossed. Okay, we'll be leaving in ten minutes. Remember, it's a night drive, so if you have a tendency to get chilled, you might want a windbreaker of some sort."

I do, and I did. "I'm going to get a fleece. You want one?"

"I'll be fine," Alice said.

"If I get trapped by an elephant, tell 'em to wait for me."

I went back to the tent and stuck my fleece in my backpack. I stuck Alice's in too. Otherwise she'd get cold, and I'd feel obligated to give her mine.

I zipped up my backpack, went out of the tent, and ran into an elephant.

What were the odds? I'd mentioned getting trapped by an elephant as insurance against getting trapped by an elephant, and here I was, trapped by an elephant. I mean, come on. And he wasn't lumbering down to the river, he was standing in the middle of the path. He was swishing his trunk around as if sniffing the ground, and as I watched he picked up something and put it in his mouth. He repeated the motion, and that time I caught what it was. A small red crumply fruit. As soon as I realized that, I saw there were several more on the ground. And the elephant was going to stand there and eat them all until the jeeps drove off. Surely Alice wasn't going to let them leave just to teach me a lesson.

I don't know how long I might have stood there like a fool, but I heard someone call, "Here!"

I looked around. One of the porters who had taken the duffles was waving at me from the corner of the tent. I followed him down by the river, where Alice had told me not to go, and we walked parallel to the path by the front of the tents where the walls were glass and the showers had no curtains because no one ever went. I had no idea which tent was Lolita's, but I had a horror I'd walk by and find her perched on the toilet and she'd see me looking in.

That didn't happen. Instead, the elephant came around the corner of a tent and blocked our path again. At least *an* elephant came around the corner of the tent. I couldn't swear it was the same elephant. All I know is it was equally large.

We changed direction, slipped between two tents back to the path, where another elephant — and here I'm sure it was a different elephant unless the one we'd just seen could teleport — was chowing down crumpled red things.

We stopped, considered our options. Clemson hadn't said if you're trapped between two elephants which one you walk toward.

Luckily, the porter made the decision, leading me back in the direction of my tent, then veering off and crossing the path to the far side, from which we could give the elephant a wide berth.

When we finally reached the parking lot, everyone else was already in the jeeps. There were two of them, the ones we'd taken from the airport, with room for a guide and a driver and six passengers in each. The pairings were shaken up a little. The married couple, the two women, and the two men were in one jeep, the women in front, the couple in the middle, and the men in back.

In my jeep, Lolita and her mother sat in the seat behind the driver, the older woman travelling alone sat in the middle, and Alice-whose-husband-had-been-trapped-by-an-elephant sat in back.

"Ah, good, you found him," Clemson said.

"We were playing elephant tag," I said. "I was going to just move them out of the way, but you said not to, so we went around."

"Are you going to get in?" Alice said.

I climbed up next to Alice. It was a little harder climbing up into the back. Still, I was glad she'd chosen that seat instead of the one behind Lolita.

The porter who'd come to get me jumped up in the seat beside our driver, confusing me as to the young man's function. If the other man was the driver, was he the guide?

"All set," Clemson said. He climbed up next to the woman traveling alone, and we took off, jouncing along the dirty pile of ruts that passed for a road.

The driver turned in his seat, flashed a big smile, and said, "I am your guide. My name is John. That is Daniel. He is our spotter. He will be looking for things I can't see because I must pay attention to my driving."

John was paying no attention to his driving, he was looking at us, and we were heading for a large tree.

Clemson didn't seem particularly concerned. "You are very lucky," he said. "John is one of our best guides."

John acknowledged the compliment and managed to miss the tree. We bounced along, looking for game. There was none. Despite what Clemson might say, apparently all the elephants lived in camp.

There were, however, a zillion birds, which John pointed out with great delight. He would slam the jeep to a halt, nearly catapulting us out of our seats, snatch up his binoculars, point, and declare triumphantly, "Lilac-breasted roller!"

At first this was annoying, because by the time I was able to figure out what he was pointing at and aim my binoculars at it, the jeep would have taken off again. Alice, on the other hand, would not only have been able to spot the Northern Carmine Bee-eater, for instance, but would have focused the long lens on it and snapped off a few dozen pix. But after a while, when I was actually finding a White-throated Blue Swallow or two, it was kind of fun.

I still would have traded them all for one mangy lion.

Alice didn't get tired of the birds, but she got tired of holding the camera. "Is there a sandbag?" she asked Clemson. She had learned online that supporting the long lens with a sandbag was a big help.

"Should be." He glanced around. "There's one."

The older woman sitting next to him fished it out of the well in front of her seat and handed it to Alice.

"Thanks," Alice said. "I don't believe we've met. I'm Alice."

The woman smiled. "Oh, really? I'm Alice too."

"Oh," Alice said. She smiled, but I wasn't sure she was happy having someone appropriate her name.

"Hello, Alice 2," I said. "I'm Stanley 1."

We laughed good-naturedly and went back to bird-spotting.

Lolita and her mother did not join in the fun. Nor did they seem interested in the birds. Lolita barely raised her binoculars, even for the African Fish Eagle. She seemed moody.

Before sundown we stopped at an idyllic spot overlooking the river.

"Perfect or what?" Clemson said as we

60

climbed out of the jeeps. "We'll have our cocktails and watch the sun go down."

The guides pulled out coolers and began setting up tables for a bar in the bush.

"See?" Clemson said. "All the comforts of home. With one exception. There are no restrooms at this particular facility. In the bush we emulate the animals in this respect. We mark our territory. You know about that, right? The animals pee on bushes to mark the boundaries of their domain. It's called marking their territory. So, in case anyone wants to mark their territory we have a very nice thicket of bushes. You can use that if it isn't dangerous."

"How can you tell?" one of the women said.

"We send Daniel in. If a lion eats him, it's dangerous."

I was beginning to like Clemson more.

Daniel wasn't eaten, and the bush proved popular. We used it politely, one at a time.

I marked my territory and returned to the jeep where Daniel had magically materialized a bowl of water and towel to wash our hands. I washed mine and accepted a club soda with lemon.

We had our drinks and watched the sun go down. It was magnificent. Yellows and reds and oranges. A veritable kaleidoscope of colors and lights, sort of the like the sequence at the end of *2001: A Space Odyssey.* That, in my opinion, went on too long. The sunset didn't. It set quickly, with camera shutters snapping furiously. I watched and toasted it with club soda.

I was not the only one not snapping pictures. I noticed Lolita talking to the older of the two men. He didn't seem particularly interested. Or it might have been his sunglasses — he hadn't taken off the aviator shades, even though it was getting dark. But he wasn't bending down or leaning in to talk to her. I wondered if he was gay.

I didn't see Mommy. She must have been in the bush marking her territory, creating a rare window of opportunity. I was surprised the young stud hadn't taken advantage of it.

Turned out he had. As I watched, he came back from the bar with two glasses of wine, one of which he handed to Lolita. In the gathering dark I could see her eyes light up as she accepted the wine. Subtlety, he managed to squeeze himself in between her and the other man. And he touched her occasionally. Nothing overt or suggestive, like an arm around her waist or her shoulders; he would just lightly touch her elbow while making a point. He did it several more times before Mommy returned from the bush to intervene.

Even as he turned away, I could see the smug smile on his face, and I realized what he'd been doing.

Marking his territory.

8
NIGHT DRIVE

Daniel had a spotlight. It was handheld, and he swiveled it in all directions as John bounced the jeep along.

For a while we saw nothing. Then we began spotting deer. The first indication was the gleam of their eyes as the spotlight hit them. Daniel never kept the light on their eyes, however; he always moved it quickly away. That seemed very respectful of Mother Nature and all, but I wondered how we were ever supposed to see anything.

Eyes gleamed closer to the ground. The beam stayed on. John slammed the jeep to a stop. "Genet!"

I thought he said genek and would continue to mispronounce the animal's name until someone corrected me. The genek or genet was a small furry animal with a black-and-gold spotted coat and a very long tail.

Daniel kept it in the spotlight until it ran into the bush. No one snapped pictures, there wasn't time.

"What's a genek?" I said.

"It's like a mongoose," Clemson said.

That might have been more helpful if I'd ever seen a mongoose. Fortunately, one showed up not long after the genet. He too was shy about performing in the spotlight, so the glimpse was brief. It was also disappointing. The mongoose looked like a less colorful genet. I seemed to remember they killed cobras. If so, they probably did it just to get noticed.

Minutes later the beam picked up another genet.

"Genek!" I cried, demonstrating my keen eyes and bad ears.

"Genet number 2!" Clemson declared as it scurried off into the darkness. "Mowangi saw nine last week. We might beat that!"

I was sorry to hear it. A fierce interest in how many genets we might see seemed like a ploy to distract us from the fact we weren't going to see anything bigger.

Wrong again.

We bounced around a bend and there was a hippo.

It was huge, though not like an elephant. Of course, I was seeing him from the highest seat in the jeep. If you haven't seen elephants on the ground, trust me, the experience is not comparable.

At any rate, the hippo didn't seem bothered by the light. He was, after all, a hippo. He stood there calmly, while the cameras clicked.

"Is that unusual?" I said.

"What?"

"To see a hippo out of water."

Clemson shook his head. "They come out at night to eat."

"What do they eat?"

"Sausage fruit," Alice 2 said.

I knew about sausage fruit. John had pointed it out earlier on the afternoon drive. They grew on trees, and they looked like huge salamis, only of a greenish hue.

"How do they get them?" I said. "Bump the tree and shake them down?"

"They climb the tree." John said it with a straight face.

It took my mind a moment to process the fact he was joking. I must have looked pretty stupid.

"They cannot get them down," John said. "They find them on the ground."

I didn't recall seeing any on the ground, but given my recent track record, I wasn't going to say anything.

We found two more genets. One I mispronounced. The other someone else saw first.

Whether they mispronounced it or not, I have no idea.

We drove along, spotting small creatures and hoping for another hippo.

The jeep stopped. And there was something different about the way it stopped this time. Instead of slamming to a halt, it glided to a halt very quietly.

John held up his hand as if to forestall questions. He pointed to the bushes and whispered, "Leopard!"

Sure enough, there in the bush, in the indirect light of Daniel's beam, were glowing eyes. As my vision adjusted to the light level, the animal took shape. I could see the ears, the nose, the mouth. The black, mottled spots on the yellow coat.

I wondered if there was enough light for Alice to shoot. Alice might have wondered too, but it certainly wasn't stopping her. She fired off shot after shot.

The other jeep glided to a stop next to ours. That was a surprise. First to see it, and then to realize it hadn't been with us since we left. Of course there was no point following right behind us, Daniel's light would drive away the game, making their spotter's light moot. But like magic they showed up the minute there was a leopard.

The young man was standing in the jeep.

I wondered if that was so he could see better, or to let Lolita see him better. She looked over and he waved.

The leopard took off. One minute it was there, the next it was gone.

Clemson muttered something under his breath.

"I thought it was going to come out," Alice 2 said.

"It was," he said.

John and the other guide began talking to each other in Swahili. At least I thought it was Swahili. It turns out there's hundreds of dialects, and I had no idea which one this was. But I gathered from the body language that John shared Clemson's opinion that it was the arrival of the second jeep that had scared the leopard away. Though I'd have given some credit to the young man's cheery wave. I'm sure neither of the men said so. The guests can do no wrong.

We drove off, leaving the other jeep behind. We saw some more genets, but after the leopard they seemed tame. Even John lost his enthusiasm pointing out genet number 5. As the number increased, the exclamation mark seemed to fade away.

It was getting cold, and I was glad to have my fleece. I pulled it out of the backpack, put it on.

Alice shivered.

"Want a fleece?" I asked her.

"I'm not going to take your fleece."

I pulled it out of the backpack. "You want yours?"

"I told you not to bring that."

"Yeah, but you married a moron who can't do anything right."

Alice accepted the fleece grudgingly. She wasn't about to concede the right to blame me for bringing it.

Two genets, one mongoose, and a Spotted Eagle Owl later — the owl, I thought, was a particularly good find, sitting motionless in a tall tree, its camouflaged feathers almost indistinguishable from the bark, only its bright eyes giving it away — John pulled the jeep to a stop, pointed, and said, "Two!"

I was not impressed. Two more genets might bring us closer to the magic number, but I had no money down on the proposition, and whether we exceeded nine genets on our drive was not a real nail-biter for me.

When you're wrong, you're wrong. Daniel wasn't swiveling the light at escaping genets, he was aiming it into a gulley that ran across the field perpendicular to the road.

I followed the beam of light and gasped. It was far away and hard to see, but there did indeed appear to be two leopards down in the gully.

Before I could raise my binoculars, the jeep took off, leaving the road and bouncing across the open field toward our quarry.

"It's not two leopards," Clemson said.

I gasped. Clemson was right. It was one leopard, and what looked like a large, ferocious wolf.

"Hyena," John said, turning around in the front seat.

I got the impression our guide resented Clemson usurping his authority.

I also got the impression we were going to die as the jeep hurtled toward the gulley.

John turned just in the nick and brought us back from the brink. He snatched up the microphone from the jeep's radio, pressed the button, and said something in dialect.

The jeep slowed and we coasted to a stop not ten yards from the leopard and hyena.

They were not alone. There had a deer with them. The deer was not a friend. The deer was dead. His belly had been ripped open, and blood and entrails were oozing out on the ground. The hyena, his mouth already red with blood, was ripping at the flesh.

The leopard crouched in the shadows a short distance away.

"The leopard killed the impala, and the hyena stole it from him," Clemson said.

Ah. So the deer was an impala. I was glad I hadn't called it a deer. "Why doesn't the leopard take it back?" I said.

"You see the jaws on the hyena?"

I heard, more than saw anything. The hyena was biting down. Bones were crunching.

"He could snap the leopard in half. And the leopard knows it."

The other jeep slid to a stop in back of ours. John must have called them.

Spotlights lit up the scene. Cameras came out, exposures were discussed, shots were taken. I even got out the video camera. I wasn't sure if there was enough light to film, but it was worth a try.

A commotion from the other jeep turned my head. Apparently the young man had gone a little heavy on the sundowners. He was giving the driver a hard time for stopping behind our jeep, where he couldn't see as well.

The other passengers in the jeep seemed torn between being embarrassed by this display, and wanting to have a better view. After a few moments the beleaguered driver started the motor, drove around us, and parked the jeep right in our path.

Clemson was furious. He didn't say anything, at least nothing we could hear.

The proximity of the jeep didn't scare the hyena away. From the look of things, nothing short of a bomb blast was going to scare the hyena away. The leopard retreated a short distance, but hung out hopefully.

We hung out too, our vision partly impaired, and rooted for the leopard.

Eventually it managed to slip in, steal away with what appeared to be the stomach. It dragged it out of sight of the hyena and began ripping it apart. Even in the dark, it was incredibly messy and gross.

Shortly after that, we headed back to camp. According to Clemson, the scene wasn't likely to change, and it was time for dinner.

I was surprisingly hungry.

9
Malarone

One problem with going to Africa is you can get malaria. Mosquitos carry it. I learned that the hard way. No, not by being bitten. By making an injudicious remark. There were flies buzzing about the jeep, and I said, "Are those tsetse flies? It would be just my luck to get malaria." Alice jumped all over me. Tsetse flies don't carry malaria. As any four-year-old knows, they carry sleeping sickness. I was not in a position to poll four-year-olds on the validity of this assertion, which I sincerely doubted — not that tsetse flies carried sleeping sickness, that four-year-olds knew it — so I let it go, as I let go more and more subjects in my declining years.

Anyway, the thing about malaria is you don't want it. You take pills so you won't get it. Or if you do get it, it will be mild. The pill you have to take is Malarone, and it's not like a vaccine you take once and you're good to go. You take pills every day of the trip, and you start two days before and end two days after, just to bookend your malaria, so to speak.

Malarone is not a high-profile drug that advertises on TV, you know, with the couple doing yard work around the house and the voiceover, "You're in the prime of your life and she's looking awful good, and you'd like to be set to go, but, hey, you've got malaria. What a bummer. Don't let malaria slow you down. Ask your doctor about Malarone. Malarone can keep you malaria-free so when she's ready, you're ready. Malarone: it keeps you good to go."

The commercial, of course, would come with the usual horrifying disclaimer, inevitably suggesting far worse results than the condition it was called upon to treat. "Warning. Consult your doctor before taking Malarone. Not all patients on Malarone are necessarily fit for sexual activity. Discontinue immediately in the event of seizure, stroke, or heart failure. Patients on Malarone may experience drowsiness, itchiness, rash, irritability, and diarrhea."

Of course, I'm making all that up. Of those symptoms, the only one I can attest to is diarrhea. Which is why I didn't go on the afternoon game hike. I figured there were no bathrooms in the bush, and there was some territory I just didn't want to mark.

Alice was gung ho for the hike. It was, after all, what it was all about. After a full day of seeing animals from the jeep, she wanted to see them up close.

It was the following day. We'd spent the morning on a game drive, uneventful, had our last lunch at elephant camp, and headed out for bush camp.

Bush camp was just what it sounded like, camp in the bush with no amenities, just small, double-occupancy tents with the sides rolled up during the day because of the heat and mosquito netting on the sides because of malaria. There was no electricity or plumbing, just a single communal outhouse in a rectangular tent slightly larger than an upright coffin. Clemson pointed it out, referring to it proudly as the straight-drop toilet.

I stayed behind when Alice left on game hike, and I spent the afternoon making use of the straight-drop toilet. I liked the straight-drop toilet. For one thing, it had a seat. For another, it didn't flush. I am suspicious of primitive toilets that flush. I always have a feeling they won't, leaving me with the prospect of taking off the back and trying to jiggle the toggle, if it's that type of toilet, or carrying buckets of water from the sink and pouring it in, never possible, or sneaking away and hoping someone else gets blamed for it.

The straight-drop toilet wasn't designed to flush. It was a hole in the ground, dug down about four feet, which, added to the height of the toilet itself, made for fairly decent straight drop down to the bottom.

Next to the toilet was a barrel of sand and a shovel. What you had to do was lift the toilet seat, take a shovelful of sand, and drop it down the hole and cover the bottom with a fresh layer of sand. The straight-drop toilet was a giant kitty litter box for people.

The walking safari wasn't home by dark. I knew they'd have to be soon, because it was dangerous. Granted, they had a jeep within hailing distance in case anyone got too tired and had to be picked up. But the group was supposed to walk back to camp.

I stayed in bed, continued taking my temperature, told myself for the hundredth time I didn't have malaria, just a side effect from the pills. There was a battery-powered lantern in the tent, but I saw no reason to turn it on until I had to get up. I lay in the dark, waiting for the hikers to return or my next attack of Malarone's revenge to kick in.

A light in another tent clicked on.

That was a surprise. I didn't know anyone else was in camp.

It was Lolita. She must have been sleeping. She had just reached up and switched on her lantern. The side flaps of her tent were up, and with the light on I could see her plain as day through the filmy mosquito netting. She was sitting up and stretching like a cat. She reached down, rummaged through her duffle, and pulled out a sweater.

It must have gotten cold when the sun went down. I hadn't really noticed. Did that mean I had fever? I was wearing a long-sleeved safari shirt. She was wearing a short-sleeved one. So she'd notice it more. Even so, maybe I should take my temperature again.

She unbuttoned her shirt and took it off. Which caught me flatfooted. I thought she was just going to pull on her sweater. She unsnapped her bra and took it off too.

My god! A bare-breasted Lolita! My most fervent hope and deepest dread! And in the feverish flash of a malaria high, I was instantly transformed into the stereotypical dirty old man, famed in song and story.

You know the last thing in the world I

wanted at that moment? Neither did I, until it happened.

Alice poked her head into the tent and said, "Guess what I saw!"

10

LEOPARD

No, Alice hadn't seen me goggling gooney-eyed at the bare breasts of my teenage dream.

Alice had seen a leopard.

It was a young leopard, and it was up a tree with its kill. They'd startled it, and it had dropped the impala, jumped down, and scurried off into the bushes with it. Alice was concerned, because that would leave it vulnerable to lions. I'd have been more concerned if there were any.

The leopard, according to John, was too young to have killed the impala himself. Mommy had done it and left it with him in the tree. She was nowhere in sight, and now there was a young leopard at large with no one to protect him.

Alice was so caught up in her leopard story, it was a while before she asked me how I felt. That was just as well. It gave me time to recover from nearly being exposed as a peeping tom.

"I feel better," I said. "But I think I'm forming a bond with the straight-drop toilet."

"Did you take Pepto-Bismol?"

"I was going to take Imodium, but I couldn't find it."

"Moron. Then you can't go to the bathroom."

"Isn't that the point?"

"No. You just want to be normal, not constipated."

"How can I be normal if I've got malaria?"

"You haven't got malaria."

"I've got diarrhea. Isn't that a symptom of malaria?"

"That's a side effect of Malarone. Symptoms of malaria don't show up until a week after you're bitten."

"Maybe I got bitten in New York."

"Don't be dumb."

Alice flopped the backpack down on the bed, pulled out the camera. "Wanna see my pictures?"

"Can I wait until I feel better?"

"Suit yourself." Alice looked around for the lantern. "Why don't you have the light on?"

"I was asleep."

"You were sitting on the bed."

"I woke up."

Alice turned on the lantern. "And sat there in the dark?"

"I was making a value judgment. Whether to go back to the straight-drop toilet."

"What did you decide?"

"I'm still on the fence."

"Not a good place for a person with diarrhea."

Alice got out her cable and plugged the camera into the iPad. Pictures began loading. I couldn't see, from where I was, but she seemed satisfied.

"I was talking to one of the women."

"Oh?"

"The sisters who are traveling together."

"They're sisters?"

"Yes. Couldn't you tell?"

No, I couldn't. For my money, they looked like refugees from a biker bar.

"Anyway, I was talking to the older one."

"Did she tell you she's older?"

"No."

"But you could tell?"

"Can't you?"

"Alice."

"She's having a hard time."

"With what?"

"With her sister."

"Why?"

81

Alice shook her head. "She made me promise not to tell."

"I'm your husband."

"I *know* you're my husband."

"Did she really expect you not to tell me?"

"She doesn't know us."

"So?"

"Lots of wives don't tell their husbands things."

"I'm glad to hear it."

"Stanley."

I took a breath. "Alice, I have a fever. I've been lying in my tent all day while you've been chasing leopards. Frankly, my head is coming off. You brought it up. Why'd you even mention it if you weren't going to tell me?"

"She's a nymphomaniac."

"What?"

"She has to watch her all the time to keep her away from men."

"*That* woman is a nymphomaniac?"

"You don't even know which one I'm talking about."

"What difference does it make? I can't believe either one of them's a nymphomaniac."

"You're very naïve. Anyway, if she starts flirting with you, it's not your irresistible charm."

I smiled. "Ah. Of course. So that's why you brought it up."

"What do you mean?"

"So you could get in that devastating zinger. Tell me, did you think that up on the walk?"

"No, that's the type of thing *you* do. Rehearse real life, write your lines."

"I'm glad we had this little talk."

"And you don't have a fever."

"What?"

"You said your head was coming off because you had a fever. You don't. You're cool as a cucumber."

"You haven't even checked."

Alice reached for her duffle.

"What are you doing?"

"Getting the digital thermometer."

"I've got it right here."

"So you *took* your temperature."

"Yes."

"And?"

"It was ninety-nine."

"Almost half a degree! Oh, my god! Hang in there, I'll call nine-one-one!"

"It may have gone up."

"I hope not. We don't have a defibrillator."

"You're in rare form today."

Alice picked up her iPad.

"And you're lookin' awful good."

"Hey. You're sick."

I grabbed Alice by the arm, tugged her toward the bed. "I'm not *that* sick."

"Stanley!"

"I can't help it. It was all that sexy talk about nymphomaniac biker babes."

"Biker babes?"

"You know. Girls who hang out in biker bars and fight each other with broken beer bottles."

"You think she's a Hells Angel?"

"I think *you're* a Hells Angel. A very attractive Hells Angel."

"Stanley. Stop it."

"How do you expect me to get better if I don't feel better?"

"Stanley. The light's on."

"So?"

"These are not solid walls. When the light's on, you can see right through them."

"Hadn't noticed."

11
TRACKS

"That's a lion," Alice said.

It didn't look like a lion. It looked like dried mud. "Are you sure?"

"Of course, I'm sure."

On her two-hour hike with John, Alice had become an expert on animal tracks. There was nothing I could say that was going to convince her those squiggles in the dirt weren't the paw of a lion.

"But's that right next to our tent."

"So?"

"You're saying a lion was outside our tent last night?"

"*I'm* not saying it. The *tracks* are saying it."

"If a lion had come by, don't you think we would have known?"

"You wouldn't. You were snoring like a grumpus."

"Even so."

"If you don't believe me, ask John."

Our guide was squatting over a campfire, grilling toast. The other guide was also making toast over a campfire. I wondered if that meant they were each feeding only the people in their group. That seemed silly, but didn't make it unlikely.

"He's busy," I said.

"Not too busy to answer a question."

Alice stomped off toward the campfire.

I caught up. "You're walking away from your paw print."

"You think I couldn't find it again?"

"I couldn't."

"You can barely find the tent. John?"

John looked up from the toast he was turning. "Yes?"

"I found a lion's paw print."

"Where?"

"Right outside our tent," I said.

John nodded. "Yes."

"Can you take a look and tell us if it's a lion?"

"It is a lion," John said.

"Outside our tent?"

"Yes."

"There was a lion outside our tent last night?"

"Lions came by."

"Lions!"

"Two or three."

"Did you see them?"

"I heard them. I did not get up." He indicated the fire. "Toast?"

Alice claimed the toast as her just reward for being right and moved on to the table where oatmeal was being ladled out. I followed in a daze, accepted my oatmeal like a good boy, and sat in one of the folding director's chairs arranged in a semicircle around the campfire.

Possible nymphomaniac Hells Angel number one sat down next to me.

She was the smaller but tougher-looking of the two. Her jet black hair was swept up into a perfectly acceptable 'do for a greaser. "See the lion?" she said.

"No. Did you?"

"I heard something. But the flaps were down. I wasn't about to go outside."

The mosquito net walls of our tent were just for daytime. At night you zipped the canvas flaps down for warmth and privacy. Alice and I had done it when it started to get cold. We had had, alas, no need for privacy.

"What time was that?"

"Between two and three."

"Really."

That was around the time I'd been communing with the straight-drop toilet. I nibbled a piece of toast, wondered how close I'd come to encountering a lion.

I was hoping Alice would come and sit down, because I'd know from her demeanor whether I was dealing with the nymphomaniac Hells Angel, but she was over by the coffee urn having a spirited discussion with Clemson. I figured she was educating the noted naturalist and founder of Clemson Safaris on the finer points of tracking.

I ate my toast, warmed myself by the fire.

Someone plopped down in the seat next to me. I looked around expecting to see Alice, and found myself face to face with Lolita.

I was dumbfounded. I didn't know what to say. The only thing that sprang to mind was, *You have nice tits.* Thank goodness I didn't blurt it out. A simple hi would have been appropriate, but I couldn't even manage that.

Lolita giggled. "You look like you saw a ghost."

"I'm sorry. I thought you were my wife."

"Oh, naughty boy! I hope she didn't hear you."

I smiled, hoping the same thing.

"See the lion?" she said.

"No. Did you?"

"Our tent flaps were down. You can't see

anything with the tent flaps down."

That was a line I wouldn't touch for love nor money. Luckily the young man sat on the other side of Lolita and distracted her attention.

I turned back to the potentially amorous Hells Angel, hoping either Alice or her sister would sit down next to her, but it was the other husband who pulled up a chair. He looked haggard and his eyes were bloodshot.

"Rough night?" I said.

"I couldn't sleep."

"You heard the lion?" Hells Angel #1 said.

"I heard noises. I don't know what they were."

"You didn't hear roaring?" I said.

"If I heard roaring, I'd know it was a lion. I just heard something moving around. It could have been someone using the john."

The straight-drop toilet was not my private domain, though I'd come to think of it that way when everyone else was hiking and I was in need.

"Okay," Clemson said, and I realized everyone had sat down. "We are going on safari. And right off the bat we've got something to track. There were lions in camp last night. We don't know how fast they're going, or how far they've gone. But we're going to find out. We'll set out from here right after breakfast. We'll stop for mid-morning tea. We'll be back here between eleven and twelve for lunch. Yesterday we hiked in late afternoon and the sun wasn't that hot. Today it will be. You'll need a hat and sunscreen. Make sure you take your own water bottle. They have your names written on them in magic marker. They'll be refilled and on that table."

The bottles, which hung around your shoulder on a canvas strap, hadn't been important in the jeep, where bottles of water were readily available. After breakfast, I picked up ours from the table. Mine was simply marked Stanley. Alice's was marked Alice H., so as not to confuse it with Alice 2.

We set off right after breakfast. Even without the jeeps, we were two separate groups. The tour guides were responsible for no more than six hikers at a time.

The guides were not alone. In addition to the spotter, each guide had a ranger with a rifle in the party. Despite never having been a huge NRA supporter, I was glad.

Clemson had shuffled the groups. I gathered that was the plan, to switch around so everyone went with everyone else. Alice and I were still with John, but today the rest of our party were the married couple and the two men. Clemson and the five women went with Mowangi.

"Okay," Clemson said. "This is where we split up. We'll go this way, you go that way."

"Hey," Alice said, as Clemson's party started out. "That's the way the lions went."

"Is that right?" I said.

"That's the way the tracks went," John said. "But it does not mean the lions are there. They go where they want."

"But they can track them," Alice said.

"They follow paw prints in the dirt. Then the grass gets thick."

"And they can't find the prints?" I said.

"Yes." John held up one finger, smiled. "We will see a lion first."

"Before them?"

He nodded. "We will see one first."

The young man, who had seemed moody, probably at being separated from Lolita, perked right up. "Then let's go," he said.

He pushed by me and I saw the name on his water bottle. Keith. Lolita's young suitor was Keith. I didn't like Keith.

We set out from camp on a dirt road in the opposite direction from which Clemson had gone.

Alice walked ahead of me, studying the ground. "Here's some tracks," she said.

John stopped, turned back. "Yes, that is a lion."

"Can we follow them?" I said.

"Don't be dumb," Alice said. "See the front toes? The lion is going that way, back to camp."

I swallowed my ignominy, tagged along quietly. Hoped if we did find a lion, the ranger wouldn't have to shoot it. Or it wouldn't eat me.

I was wearing my hat and my sunglasses. My backpack was lighter today because Alice had opted for the lighter camera. Actually it was the same camera with a shorter lens. The long lens, Alice had discovered, was just too heavy for hiking. I could thank Malarone for that decision. If I had been on the hike the night before, I might have lugged the long lens, and Alice wouldn't have felt the strain.

It turned out I didn't have to carry the lighter camera either. Alice wanted it at the ready. Having it in my backpack wouldn't do.

I had the movie camera in my backpack just in case. I wasn't counting on anything, but if a lion did chow down on one of us, I didn't want to miss it. Alice would be miffed if I did.

We didn't see any animals, but we sure

found a lot of tracks. I learned the various characteristics of each. Not that I could have passed an exam on it, but I understood. That would not likely be enough for Alice, who had mastered lion, leopard, impala, warthog, and aardvark on the afternoon hike.

I kept my eyes on the ground, hoping to spot some track Alice had missed. I'd have had a better chance of flying to the moon. The only thing that kept me from falling behind was our spotter Daniel, whose job was to bring up the rear. Today Daniel had an even younger man along, who turned out to be his apprentice.

In a clear area of the dirt path, John stopped and called us around. "See?" he said.

I looked and didn't see at all. Instead of the usual animal track, there was nothing there.

I was about to stick my neck out and say what, when Keith said it for me.

John pointed. "The hole."

I looked closer. There was indeed a hole. I hadn't seen it because it was the size of a pencil lead. It looked that way too, slightly funneled as if someone had stuck the tip of a pencil in the ground.

"Do you know what that is?"

No one did.

John took out a hunting knife I hadn't realized he was carrying, punched it into the earth next to the hole, and pried up. He sifted the dirt with his hands, smiled brightly, and pointed to his palm. Wriggling there was a tiny bug.

"Ant lion," he said proudly.

It took me a second to realize this was the lion he had promised we would find first. I was disappointed, though 'disappointed' is not the right word. 'Betrayed' seemed too harsh. But I'd been duped and I wasn't happy about it, and whatever joy there was at finding this tiny lion was totally eclipsed by the feeling he was an imposter and not at all what I'd expected.

John, meanwhile, had swung into full lecture mode, probably enjoying the freedom of being out from under Clemson's thumb. The ant lion, I was learning, had dug this funnel-shaped hole expressly for the purpose of trapping unwary ants, who never seemed to learn that this was the reason the holes were there, despite the fact that they were dug for no other purpose. I supposed the slow learning curve could be excused for the fact that the ants that did learn were eaten before they could profit from their experience.

The ant lion was a member of the Little 5, which included the buffalo weaver, a bird; the leopard tortoise, a turtle; the elephant shrew, a small, insect-eating mammal; and the rhino beetle, another bug.

The Big 5 were the lion, leopard, elephant, Cape buffalo, and rhinoceros. The giraffe was missing because the term was coined to refer to the five most dangerous game to hunt.

The Big and Little 5 were essentially just a marketing ploy to hype the tours, but that didn't stop John from waxing eloquent about the ferocious ant lion, too small to see.

"Take your binoculars," John told Alice.

Alice frowned quizzically. "You want me to look at it with binoculars?"

"Turn them around."

"Huh?"

"Turn the binoculars around. Turn them around the other way. Let the lion look at you."

"You gotta be kidding," I said.

Alice unsnapped her binoculars from the harness and turned them upside down.

"Close one eye," John said. "Look at the lion with the other eye."

Alice did as she was told, aimed the eyepiece of the binoculars at the tiny creature. "Oh, my goodness!" she said. "Stanley, it's like looking in a microscope."

"Oh, come on," I said. I took the binoculars, closed my eye, and looked.

It wasn't a microscope, but it was the next best thing. The magnification was incredible. I could actually see the damn thing. It had nasty looking pincers to do an ant in. I wondered how big an ant would look under the binoculars. It would be like the movie *Them*.

All right, it wasn't as good as a real lion, but I figured I should let John off the hook.

A little further along, John held up his hand and we stopped.

In the clearing ahead was a giraffe. He was reaching his long neck up to eat the leaves off a tree.

That was more like it. I slung the backpack off my shoulders, fumbled for the video camera. I clicked it on, focused, zoomed in.

Alice had her camera out, but she wasn't shooting anything.

"What's the matter?" I said.

"We're facing into the sun."

I wondered if that meant I shouldn't be shooting video either. I was getting a picture on my screen. I stopped filming, though. I had a shot of the giraffe eating leaves. I could turn it on again if he did something else.

"Come," John said quietly, beckoning with his hand. "Try not to scare him."

We crept across the clearing. We were fifty yards away from the giraffe and he hadn't seen us yet. I wondered how close we could get before he did.

The answer was pretty damn close. The giraffe got taller and taller as we cut the distance in half. The angle wasn't bad. Cameras were raised, shots fired.

Keith edged past Alice to get a closer shot.

The giraffe's head swiveled on its long neck, and it galloped away on long, spindly legs. Wouldn't you know it, I hadn't turned on the camera yet.

I was pissed. Not at missing the shot. At Alice missing the shot. I didn't give a damn about photography and she did. It wasn't fair that just as she got the shot lined up, the schmuck would spoil it.

The minute I had that thought, I was seized with doubt. I felt a sudden chill. It was my mind tying itself in torturous knots. Was I really angry on Alice's behalf? Or was that an automatic defense mechanism to mask my own feeling of resentment toward the young man for being successful with the young woman who was unavailable to me?

Of course, at that point it didn't matter which.

I was angry at myself just for wondering.

12
LUNCH

We never found a lion, but then neither did Clemson. Small victory there. The other group hadn't done better. Who would have thought such petty jealousies were possible? But having spent your entire life savings to get here, you wanted something more than just a bug in someone's palm.

"Where did the lions go?" I asked Alice 2 as we gathered for lunch by the river. Lunch was some chicken and rice dish. If it was African, I wouldn't have known it. I didn't care. I'd have eaten sawdust if we'd seen a lion.

"I don't know. We lost the tracks just outside of camp."

"What did you see?"

"Giraffes. Warthogs."

"We didn't see warthogs."

"They're cute in an ugly sort of way."

"Interesting way to put it," I said. "Are you a writer?"

She laughed. "Goodness, no. I'm a law-yer."

"What kind of law?"

"I'm retired now. I did corporate law. Dull, but profitable. Are you a lawyer?"

My laugh was similar to hers when I asked if she was a writer. "No. I work for one, though. Negligence lawyer."

"Oh? Who?"

"Richard Rosenberg."

"I don't know him."

"Then you're not from New York."

"Minneapolis."

"New York lawyers know him. They stay away from him."

"He's that bad?"

"He's that good. If he goes to court, he wins."

"So what did you see?"

"Giraffe. A few elephants."

Lolita's mother looked up from her chicken and rice. "We got trapped by an elephant."

I was surprised. Not that an elephant had trapped them. But the woman was talking to me, and in a friendly, conversational way, rather than regarding me as pond scum. I'd avoided the empty seat between the two women when I sat down, and not just to leave room for my wife.

"Really," I said. "So you went around him?"

"That wasn't an option," Alice 2 said.

Lolita's mother concurred. "No. He'd seen us. He was interested. When that happens, you can't run or he'll charge."

"What did you do?"

"It was scary. Sampson cocked his gun."

I assumed Sampson was their ranger. "Really?"

"He wasn't going to shoot him," Alice 2 said. "Just fire in the air and scare him."

"I didn't hear a shot."

"He didn't have to. Clemson clapped his hands and drove him away."

"But it was scary," Lolita's mother persisted. "When he ran at us."

"The elephant charged you?" I said.

"It was nothing. Sampson threw the bolt and Clemson clapped his hands." Alice 2 lowered her voice. "Mowangi wasn't happy. About Clemson taking charge."

"He had to," Lolita's mother said. "The elephant was coming right at us! Right at us!" She seemed to be getting worked up as she relived the incident. I wondered if it was for her or for her daughter she was scared.

As if on cue, Lolita plunked herself down

in the empty seat. "What are you talking about?"

"That awful elephant."

"The elephant was fine. We weren't in any danger."

"Sampson thought we were. He cocked his gun."

"He said why. He wasn't going to shoot the elephant. He was going to shoot in the air."

"I don't like guns."

Ah. Another non NRA supporter. In her case, that didn't necessarily make her left-wing. She probably didn't like sex, drugs, or rock and roll either.

Both Hells Angels splashed down on my right. That was okay with me. Alice hadn't even gotten her plate yet. She'd gone out to the jeep to plug in her battery charger. Bush camp had no charging station, in fact no electric facilities of any kind. A power strip in the jeep was used for charging, and it could only handle two batteries at a time when the jeep wasn't running. At least that was the limit allowed, and I couldn't imagine anyone wanting to challenge it. A jeep with a dead battery was the last thing we needed. Even with limited use, they were taking no chances. They revved the engine a few minutes every hour to keep the battery charged.

Keith came over with a plate of food. The young man seemed miffed that the seat next to Lolita was taken. He wasn't about to sit next to Mommy. He plunked down next to Hells Angel #2. "What's this about an elephant?"

"Came right at us," Hells Angel #2 said. I wondered if she was the amorous one. She was sitting next to Keith, but then he'd sat down next to her.

"Charged by an elephant," he said. "That must have been fun." He wasn't just talking to the Hells Angels, he was talking loud enough for Lolita to hear, and glancing covetously in her direction.

Alice sat down next to Lolita's mother. "I hear you had quite an adventure with an elephant."

As Mommy turned to Alice, Lolita put her hands up in a please-not-again gesture. I bristled. It was okay for Keith to bring it up, but just let Alice horn in on the conversation. On the other hand, Alice's remark set Mommy off again, and we went through another we-were-almost-killed tirade.

Clemson pulled up a chair and chimed in as if he'd just heard his cue. "Nonsense. We were never in any danger. Clemson Safari is the safest in the world. Never had an accident, and never will." He smiled, spread his arms. "Can't afford to be sued."

He was joking, of course, but I couldn't help thinking of the suit Richard Rosenberg might file if I were killed by an elephant. "You've never had any accidents at all?" I said.

"Depends what you mean by accidents. A guy slipped climbing out of the jeep and broke his leg. We set out steps, but this was in the bush, the guy wanted to mark his territory and didn't want to wait for them. He was in a hurry and he slipped."

"And broke his leg?" I said.

"Yes."

"He still managed to mark his territory?"

"Yes, but not the territory he wanted to mark. Aside from that we've had the usual number of cuts and scrapes, but nothing serious. And no one's been hurt by an animal."

I wish he hadn't said that. You don't talk about it when a guy's throwing a perfect game. Even the sportscasters won't mention it. They'll talk all around the subject, like giving the line score, no runs, no hits, no errors, or saying the so-and-sos are looking for their first base runner, but they'll never say the pitcher's throwing a perfect game. It just isn't done. It's the biggest no-no in baseball, to jinx a pitcher throwing a perfect game by talking about it. The players wouldn't even mention it, and if they did, they wouldn't mention it to him. If you see a pitcher who has a perfect game going sitting on the bench while his team is batting, there's never anyone sitting next to him. No one will go near him. They're afraid they'll say something to inadvertently jinx the poor guy.

And one thing that will never, ever happen is the pitcher mentioning it. He won't say, *Hey, I'm throwing a perfect game.* Not unless he's the biggest arrogant schmuck to come down the pike. A mindless, clueless, muscle-bound freak, who has a good fastball and no common sense. But anyone else, he'd rather cut off his right arm than mention it. Because it is the kiss of death.

I suppose I could forgive Clemson. He was South African. Presumably never followed baseball. What did they play, cricket? They were British enough in other ways, drove on the wrong side of the road. Even so, whether he knew baseball or not, it just wasn't done.

Clemson had bragged that he was throwing a perfect game.

That couldn't be good.

13
SAUSAGE FRUIT

John couldn't find Daniel. We didn't know it at first, but that was why the next morning's hike was late. Alice and I didn't know because we were in Mowangi's group. His spotter and ranger were there, so as far as I knew we were set to go.

Clemson had pulled John and Mowangi aside and was talking to them in quiet intensity. He did not look happy, and that was saying something, because Clemson always looked happy. But the hail-fellow-well-met, this-is-my-tour-so-I-named-it-after-me was having a hard time of it, and from what I could see he was passing it along.

Eventually it filtered down to us that Daniel wasn't here. It was the wife of the other couple, whose water bottle was hanging down the wrong way so I couldn't see her name, who brought us the news. Her husband had run back to his tent for some memory, which sounds weird to me, but just means a little chip for his camera instead of a roll of film, and he had walked close enough to the group to hear what they were saying. Apparently Clemson, for all his other accomplishments, was not fluent enough in the local language and was conversing with the guides in English.

"He's blaming John," the husband said. "Isn't that a little harsh? I mean, if the kid doesn't show up on time, is that John's fault? For all he knows, the boy just wandered off."

"Wandered off where?" Lolita said. "We're in the bush. It's not like there's some card game or strip club he could wander off to."

Her mother was shocked. "Really! How can you joke? The poor young man. Something must have happened to him."

"Oh, I'm sure nothing happened to him," I said.

But I'd have felt much better about it if Clemson hadn't been bragging about his perfect game. If anything happened to Daniel, it was going to be his fault.

"I'm sure he'll show up," Alice said.

Daniel didn't show up, and his apprentice was pressed into service. I wondered if he'd be nervous. It was like the understudy going on for the star. Or to keep the baseball analogy going, like the minor leaguer being called up to the Show. Actually, it shouldn't be that hard. While spotting animals on the night drive might be an art, from what I'd seen the day before the spotter's job on the hikes was mainly being last in line so any animal sneaking up from behind would eat him first. I figured Daniel's replacement was up to the task.

Mowangi's group consisted of me and Alice, Lolita and her mother, and the two Hells Angels. Then there was Mowangi's ranger, whose name I didn't remember despite having heard it the day before, and Mowangi's spotter, also nameless. The spotter had no apprentice. I didn't know who would fill in if he ran off.

Mowangi and John mixed it up by setting off in the opposite directions from which they'd gone the day before, which was great for them, and not so much for me and Alice, who wound up going the same way we had gone with John. Mowangi didn't bother pointing out the ant lion holes. I wondered if he'd done it the day before, assuming there were ant lions in that direction.

He did point out an elephant we hadn't seen walking with John. Of course he didn't have much choice, it was right in our path. I could see Lolita's mother tense up. She must have thought the damn things were stalking her. The elephant made no attempt to charge us. He looked slightly bored. He turned and wandered away into the bush.

Behind me I could hear Alice calling the elephant names under her breath. I turned, saw that she hadn't gotten her camera out in time.

The path having been cleared, Mowangi resumed the walk.

As we started up again, I noticed Hells Angel #2 talking to Lolita. I wondered if she was the amorous one. If so, I wondered if her sister meant she was a sex-crazed lesbian. Or at least bisexual. That would figure. Lolita was enough to turn any woman bisexual.

I wanted to ask Alice if I'd correctly identified the amorous Hells Angel, but she was busy fiddling with her camera. Apparently you couldn't just point and shoot, there was a lot of fine tuning, something about f-stops and overexposures, stuff I don't understand. There's a lot of stuff I don't understand. I was born not understanding.

A short while later, Mowangi spotted an African Hawk-Eagle. It was a good spot. There were hawks and eagles listed in the field guide, but to rack up two with one blow was impressive. The Hawk-Eagle wasn't doing anything, just sleeping on a high branch, but I figured it still counted.

I was quite impressed with Mowangi's powers of observation. I wondered what the next thing would be that we would find.

I was rooting for a lion, but I wasn't holding my breath.

We came into a clearing I recognized from the day before. There was a sausage-fruit tree in it, and it was even more impressive than the one I had seen from the jeep. The sausage fruit were tremendous. They looked like salamis. And not Genoa salamis, but larger, like big bolognas. John had cautioned us not to walk under them, though the admonition was hardly necessary. I'd have sooner walked under a construction site.

There'd been no fruit on the ground then. I wondered why there were none now. They had to fall sometime. If the hippos ate them all night, they had to fall during the day. I wanted to find one on the ground, see how heavy they actually were.

So I should have seen it first, but instead it was Alice, sucking in her breath and saying, "Oh, my god!"

I saw what she was looking at, and my face froze.

It was Daniel.

He was lying facedown under the tree. A large sausage fruit lay on the ground next to him.

The back of his head was caved in.

14
CRIME SCENE

They didn't know how to handle the crime scene. I'm not a cop, so I don't know how to handle them myself, but I'd been at enough of them to know that what they were doing wasn't it.

First Mowangi rolled the body over and tried to revive him. Not that he had a prayer of doing so. Even with my limited medical training — none — I could tell that he'd been dead for hours.

Also, expert tracker that he was, Mowangi was tramping all over the place, obliterating whatever footprints there might have been in the dirt, and just generally making a hash of it.

He also whipped out a walkie-talkie I didn't know he had, and minutes later one of the jeeps came crashing through the underbrush to complicate the picture. En route they had managed to snare John, Clemson, and the other party, so we had an absolute zoo at the crime scene.

Fortunately, Clemson took charge. Unfortunately, he refused to recognize the crime scene as a crime scene. He also refused to acknowledge that Daniel was dead, pinching him, slapping him, and doubtless calling him the most unspeakable names in dialect. None roused him. The promotion of Daniel's apprentice was apparently permanent.

Clemson also picked up the sausage fruit, which answered the question of how heavy it was. From the effort it took, the answer was pretty damn heavy. I had no doubt it could have bashed in Daniel's head. I just wasn't sure it had done so.

Of course, Clemson was not the ultimate authority. The ranger was. Not Mowangi's ranger, but John's ranger, who'd gone with us the day before. Clemson declared him in charge, addressed him as Duke. I had to resist an urge to ask him if he was named after Duke Snider.

Needless to say, the violent demise of our young spotter had thrown our tour group into a state of consternation. Clemson seemed to be taking it in stride, but the rest of us weren't. Of course a sausage fruit wasn't an animal, so Clemson still had his perfect game going. Inappropriate Thought #768.

"We've had a little accident," Clemson said.

Lolita's mother was incensed. "A little accident? The boy is dead."

"That is the unfortunate result. And that is why we don't let you leave camp without a guide."

"He *is* a guide," Hells Angel #2 said. She sounded angry. I could imagine her ripping someone's head off. That gave me a little pause on her amorous designation.

"I know," Clemson said. "And he should have known better. It just goes to show you." Exactly what it meant to show us, Clemson didn't expand on. "Anyway, Phillip has filled in."

Phillip seemed an appropriate name for a fill-in. Inappropriate Thought #769.

"We all feel sorry for the boy," Clemson continued. "We'll certainly have some sort of tribute, and I'll be happy to take up a small collection for his family. For the time being, we're scrapping the morning schedule. We're all together, and we'll stay together. It's about time for our midmorning snack. We'll find a spot and set up tea and coffee in the bush."

"Midmorning snack," Lolita's mother wailed. "How can you think of eating?"

"For goodness sakes," Hells Angel #1

said. "You think not eating's going to help?"

"At any rate," Clemson said, "let's get away from here."

No one objected to getting away from the sausage-fruit tree, crime scene or not.

Daniel's body was loaded into the back of the jeep. Clemson took the driver aside to give him instructions.

I hadn't gotten a good look at the body, what with Mowangi pouncing on him and trying to cudgel him back to life. So while they were making preparations to go, I managed to sneak around to the back of the jeep and take a peek under the blanket.

I sucked in my breath.

Daniel's head wasn't caved in as if hit with a blunt object. His wound was a jagged gash.

There was no way it had been made by a sausage fruit.

The jeep started up.

I dropped the blanket back in place and stepped away before anyone saw me.

We watched the jeep drive off, and left the clearing.

A five-minute walk through the brush brought us back to the river. The guides began setting out refreshments. Lolita's mother declined any sustenance, but Alice and I accepted tea and took a cookie.

I drew her off to one side. "Daniel wasn't

hit with a sausage fruit," I said. "His head was gashed open with a sharp object."

"How do you know?"

"I saw it."

"Why didn't you say anything?"

"I just saw it."

"No, you didn't. The body's gone."

"I saw it just before it drove off. I wasn't going to jump in front of the jeep and say, *Stop!* If I had, you'd have called me an idiot."

"That's never stopped you before."

"Alice."

"Are you sure about this?"

"No. But there's no way a sausage fruit could make a wound like that."

"Then you *are* sure."

"Okay, I'm sure."

"How can you be sure?"

I opened my mouth, closed it again.

"You're spilling your tea."

I looked. My tea, unheeded, was sloshing out of the cup, perilously close to my pants leg.

"What are you going to do?" Alice said.

"I'll try to hold the cup more steady."

"Stanley."

"Well, I'm not going to leap up and tell everyone I'm a private investigator and I think there's been a murder."

116

"I'm glad to hear it. So what will you do? Tell Clemson?"

"I'll tell Duke."

"Why not Clemson?"

"He won't admit it wasn't an accident. He doesn't want his tour shut down for a murder investigation."

"That's not his choice."

"It is until someone in authority tells him it isn't."

The tea had been handed out and people were conversing in small groups. Clemson was talking to John, who apparently was taking the loss of his spotter hard. Duke was standing off to the side. He appeared lost in thought.

I went over and said, "Excuse me."

He looked up as if he couldn't believe I was talking to him. I hadn't heard him talk to anyone but John. I wondered if he spoke English.

"I need to talk to you about Daniel," I said.

He looked at me, said nothing. I couldn't tell if he understood me.

"Do you think he was hit with a sausage fruit?"

He nodded. "Sausage fruit."

"It didn't look like a sausage fruit."

"Sausage fruit."

Oh, dear. "Yes. I saw the sausage fruit on the ground. But Daniel's head did not look like it was hit with a sausage fruit. Daniel's head was cut open. Like it was hit with something sharp."

"Sausage fruit."

"Sausage fruit is not sharp. He was hit with something sharp. So he was not hit with a sausage fruit."

I could see his mind whirling as he tried to process the English. Finally he nodded. "Sausage fruit."

Clemson was finishing up his conversation. I managed to head him off. "So what's going to happen to Daniel?"

"What do you mean?"

"Is a doctor going to see him?"

"That will do no good."

"To pronounce him dead. Fill out a death certificate."

"Oh."

"Will they do that?"

"I'm sure they will."

That's what I expected him to say. It's the kind of answer that freely translated means I have no idea. I might have posed a follow-up, but having delivered that equivocal assessment, Clemson moved on.

I might have tried John, but he was busy reassuring Daniel's replacement that the position wasn't necessarily a dead-end job.

"Leave her alone!"

It was an indignant, bordering-on-hysterical shriek. I didn't have to guess who that was. I looked up. So did everyone else in camp.

Lolita's mother had imposed herself between her daughter and Keith like an avenging fury. Keith looked sheepishly amused, but Lolita looked murderous.

Bad choice of words.

15
REHASH

Lunch was back in camp. No one ate much. No one said much. Despite Clemson's valiant attempt to carry on as if nothing had happened, we were all subdued.

After lunch, I paid tribute to the straight-drop toilet and went back to my tent.

Alice was waiting to pounce. I hadn't had a chance to talk to her alone, and she was ready to explode. "Well?"

"Well what?"

"Daniel. What did Duke say?"

"Sausage fruit."

"What did he say when you told him it wasn't?"

"Sausage fruit."

"Stanley."

"Alice, there's a language barrier. I told him Daniel's wound was not consistent with being struck with a blunt object. He said sausage fruit. It's hard to argue with that."

"But —"

"I don't know the camp staff, I don't even know how many there are. I only know Daniel's replacement because he was along on the walk. But the guys who set up camp and cook and bring the hot water, I have no idea."

"So you're not going to do anything?"

"There's nothing to do."

Alice said nothing, just looked at me.

"What do you want me to do?"

"I don't know."

"And yet you blame me for not doing it."

"I'm not blaming you."

Oh, dear. A familiar phrase, and one from which there was no escape. Alice said she wasn't blaming me. Which meant she was blaming me. But since she said she wasn't, there was nothing to push against. All I could do was sit there in the shame of my blame, and try to think my way out of it. In most cases, an impossible task. And yet our marriage endures.

Alice, having beaten me to a standstill, whipped out her iPad and began downloading pictures. I didn't realize she'd taken any this morning. I wondered if they were of the crime scene. Realized that was ridiculous. Alice hadn't even known it *was* a crime scene until I told her about the wound in his head. She'd thought he'd been hit by a sausage fruit, just like everybody else. No, these would be the pictures she took before we found him. I was glad she had. It was good she had something to occupy herself with. I wished I had some footage to look at, but I hadn't shot a thing.

A shadow blotted out the sun. I looked up. Clemson stood in the tent opening. "Listen," he said. "About Daniel."

"Sausage fruit," I said. I felt a bit of malicious glee at throwing their own game back at them.

Clemson wasn't deflected. "You were asking about it."

"Yes, and you said you didn't know."

"No, you were asking Duke. He said you were suggesting the boy's death wasn't an accident."

"I merely said the gash on his head wasn't consistent with being hit with a blunt object."

"A blunt object like a sausage fruit."

"Yes."

"If he wasn't hit with a sausage fruit, his death wasn't an accident."

"What are you implying?"

Clemson frowned. "*I'm* not implying anything. It's what *you're* implying."

"Is that what Duke said?"

"Yes, it is."

"Interesting."

"Why?"

"From what he said to me, I wouldn't have known it."

"What did he say to you?"

"Sausage fruit."

Clemson took a breath. "Duke is not particularly communicative with the tourists. He talks to me."

"Then you can discuss this with him."

"I did."

"And?"

Clemson stopped, took a breath. I could see his mind going, reminding himself I was a tourist. That telling me off was not in his best interests.

Alice, who had been restraining herself with an effort, couldn't stand it anymore. "Oh, for goodness sakes. He's a private investigator. He's been involved in murder cases. He's been around too many crime scenes to ignore a glaring inconsistency like this. The kid wasn't hit with a sausage fruit. He knows it, you know it, I know it, Duke knows it. Stop acting like he's made a major faux pas by pointing it out."

Clemson opened his mouth, closed it again, smiled. "That's very well put."

"You wouldn't want to argue with her," I observed.

"All right, look," Clemson said. "Here's the situation. This is not New York. Duke is not a homicide detective. He's a park ranger. The only homicide he ever solved was an ivory poacher shot to death in front of witnesses by a villager who bragged about it to anyone willing to listen. The Daniel situation is unfortunate. If Duke declares it a murder, he's gotta investigate it. Which means giving up this plum assignment shepherding the hikes. He likes going on the hikes. He's getting paid as a ranger, *and* he's getting paid by me. He doesn't have to do anything except carry a gun and look competent. He's never shot anything. Not in all the time he's worked for me. I don't know if his gun's even loaded." Clemson realized he'd gone too far. "I'm kidding, of course. But this is a nice job, and he's eager to do it. You think he wants to give all that up and start questioning people about a homicide? No one's gonna talk to him if they know why he's asking. Then when he can't solve it, it's an ugly unsolved crime hanging over his head and that of the other park rangers. But if it's an accident, it's a win-win. If it's never solved, no one's upset. But if the guy who did it is foolish enough to talk about it, wow. Duke can arrest him, and he'll be a big hero, solving a murder case everyone thought was an accident." He smiled ingratiatingly. "See what I mean?"

"I see what you mean, but —"

"Good. So if I can count on your discretion not to rile up the others. I doubt if any of them have had the same experience you have, and they're not going to take it as well."

"Of course not," Alice said. "Well, thanks for explaining the situation."

"No problem," Clemson said. A curious choice of words. Clearly, it was a problem. "Can I count on your discretion?"

"Absolutely," I assured him.

Clemson looked relieved. He nodded, bowed himself out of the tent.

The minute the flap closed, Alice turned to me. "Well, what are you going to do now?"

16
STAFF CAMP

I headed for the straight-drop toilet, de-
toured around it, and headed into the bush.
I had no idea what was out there behind
the toilet. It might have been the tents of
the camp crew, for all I knew. I had no idea
where they hung out. As far as I could tell,
it was just underbrush. I went in far enough
so as not to be seen, then worked my way
around to the trail.

At least that was my intention. The problem was, the trail wasn't a trail. We'd been
following some tracks in the dirt. That was
a long time and many animals ago. When I
did find some dirt, there'd be animal tracks
in it, but were they the tracks I'd seen this
morning, or other animals entirely? I had
no idea.

Was I far enough around the camp? My
intention was to travel in a huge semicircle.
I weaved my way in and out of bushes and
around trees, at the same time avoiding a

seemingly endless supply of elephant poop. I was really winging it. Of course I could take my bearings from the sun. Assuming I could remember where the sun had been this morning. And calculated how far it would have traveled by now. I forged my way through the underbrush looking for a familiar landmark.

I found one, but it didn't help. I came walking into a clearing and a giraffe reared up in front me. I don't mean on its hind legs like a stallion. It was just standing there, but it was damn high. I looked up and thought, oh, boy.

Clemson had not given us a primer on giraffes, probably because he never expected us to get this close to one. So what was the protocol? Did I say excuse me, and back deferentially into the bush? Probably, but I never got the chance. The giraffe turned and ran. Which looks great, by the way, a giraffe galloping on those long legs.

If the giraffe was going that way, I figured I should probably go the other way. I set off through the bush, being a little more careful about turning corners.

I don't know how long I might have bumbled along looking for tracks in the dirt if I hadn't happened to look up to see if I was bumping into a warthog, and seen the sausage-fruit tree. Of course it didn't have to be *the* sausage-fruit tree. It was just *a* sausage-fruit tree. But by then I was happy to find anything.

I was embarrassed to discover that even after a careful perusal, I was unable to tell if it was the right tree. Of course the last time I was here, if it was indeed here, there had been that confusion of people and bodies and jeeps. I should have been able to find evidence of that, but I couldn't, which didn't bode well for my career as a tracker, if I couldn't even find a damn jeep.

I searched all around the tree. It was only when I got to the side that I was sure it wasn't, that it turned out it was. After that, it was short work to figure out where the body had lain. I even found the sausage fruit. It was a wonder some animal hadn't come along and eaten it. I examined it for blood. Found none. The sausage fruit was bashed in. And the dent was in the bottom, which would have been hanging down, and would have been the part to strike someone if it had indeed had. It was easy to tell it was the bottom, because the vine from which it had hung was still attached. It had snapped about a foot from where it joined the fruit. All nice and kosher, as if that was the way it had happened. All of which seemed to support a theory of accidental death.

Now, then. In support of an opposing viewpoint.

I found nothing. Absolutely nothing. I don't know what I was hoping for. A lead pipe with blood on it. Signs of a struggle. I don't know what signs I was hoping for. A neon sign flashing STRUGGLE would have been nice.

My god, I'd been at it forever. I had to get back to camp for the afternoon walk. Assuming I could find camp. Of course I could. I knew where the camp was in relation to the tree and the sausage fruit. If no one had moved the sausage fruit, the camp was practically on a perpendicular with the line between them. I sighted an imaginary line and took off.

I was back in ten minutes. Feeling pretty damn proud about finding the camp, and pretty bummed out about not finding the evidence.

Now, to maneuver around as if I was just coming back from the straight-drop toilet. I circled the camp and ran straight into an elephant. I was beginning to get a complex. By now I was an old hand at this game. You didn't argue with an elephant, you just went around him. I skirted the elephant by a circuitous and serpentine route, which got me utterly lost again.

Just as I was beginning to despair, I spotted an old friend. The straight-drop toilet, shining like a beacon in the afternoon sun. Which I realized was only me projecting — the damn thing was made of canvas and did not gleam — but it sure felt that way. Only when I got closer, something seemed wrong. Suddenly I realized this wasn't our toilet. I don't know how I knew that. If questioned on the witness stand, or worse, by Alice, I couldn't point to a single characteristic, like a rip in the canvas, or a distinctive wood support, or the angle of the flap of the door that alerted me to the fact this wasn't our toilet, but I knew.

As I drew closer, I could see the tents behind it. They weren't our tents either. Had I gotten completely turned around and stumbled on another campsite altogether? No, of course not. This was our campsite. It was the unseen part. The tents of the staff. And their straight-drop toilet. Just like ours. Only not. An identical twin.

The good news was I had found our camp. The bad news was it was isolated from the main camp, and I didn't know the layout. I had no idea in what direction our tents lay.

I looked around for someone to ask, but not speaking the language, I wasn't sure anyone would be able to tell me.

I strolled around the camp but there was no one there. Out on some afternoon chore, no doubt. Getting ready for the hike.

I needed to use the straight-drop toilet. I wondered if I should infringe on their privacy, or pee in the bushes. I was heading away from the toilet. The bushes seemed a better choice. As long as I didn't pee on a lion.

I was checking the underbrush for predators when something caught my eye. A wooden stick about the size of a baseball bat. It was rough and irregular with jagged edges. Sunlight reflected off it gave off a reddish glow.

I told myself I was just imagining things. I mean, come on. Of all the gin joints in all the jungle, the murder weapon wanders into mine?

I crept closer, bent to look. Sure enough, that was blood.

I wasn't going to make the same mistake as Duke, contaminating the evidence all to hell. I did not touch the cudgel. I let it lie exactly where it was, and looked around so I could find it again. The stick was ten yards from the nearest tent on a straight line perpendicular to the back of the tent in practically the dead center. Did the tent in question have any distinguishing marks? Yes, it did. The side flap was half-up and half-down. The front half of the flap was rolled up and tied at the top with a canvas tie. The tie on the back half had come loose, allowing the flap to unroll. I came closer and saw why. One of the canvas ties was ripped off.

That was enough to identify the tent. Now to double-check that having found it, I could find the stick again.

No problem. Taking my bearings from the tent, I walked right to it.

Now if I could just find my way back to camp.

I walked through the staff camp to make sure there wasn't another tent with a flap half-down, which there didn't seem to be.

One of the staff men came out of his tent. It was Daniel's replacement, the young spotter apprentice who had taken over his job. He seemed surprised to see me. I could understand why. This was not the tourists' part of camp.

"I'm lost," I said. "Which way is camp?"

He pointed me through the bushes in a way I would not have gone if left to my own devices. I went through a thicket and emerged on the other side of our campsite, proving that the two campsites were side by side, just invisible from each other. To the right was the clearing where the jeeps were parked. To the left was the river. Straight ahead were the tents.

John was stacking wood for the campfire. I went up to him and said, "Where's Clemson?"

He looked around, said "Tent."

"Take me to him."

John was startled that I was so abrupt, but he stood up and said, "Come."

We found Clemson sitting in front of his tent, going over a ledger. At least I assumed it was some sort of ledger. It was a bound book, and he had a ballpoint pen in his hand. He looked up, frowned. Tourists clearly weren't expected at his tent.

"I found the murder weapon."

"What?"

"The stick that killed Daniel. There's blood on it. I found it."

"How did you do that?"

"I got lucky."

"I don't understand."

"Me either. I hardly ever get lucky."

"What in the world are you talking about."

"I went looking for the murder weapon. Against all odds, I found it."

"Where?"

I glanced around. John, after pointing me in Clemson's direction, had gone back to stacking firewood.

"I found it in the staff campsite."

"That's absurd."

"It's not absurd, but it certainly was a surprise."

"Why were you looking in the staff campsite?"

"Because it wasn't anywhere else."

That was as close an approximation of the truth as I wanted to give. A recitation of my misadventures could serve no earthly purpose.

"Where is this bloody stick?"

With his British accent, bloody stick sounded like a curse, which was probably how he felt about it.

"There."

"There?"

"Where I found it. I didn't touch it. I left it just where I found it so as not to contaminate the evidence."

"That seems an unnecessary precaution. I'd rather have the stick."

"Let's go get it."

"If you can find it again."

"Take me to the campsite. I'll show you where it is."

"I should tell Duke."

"Where is he?"

"I don't know." Clemson took a walkie-talkie out of his pocket, spoke into it in dialect. Seconds later it crackled, and a torrent of dialect spewed out.

"What did you tell him?" I said.

"That you're going to show us the murder weapon."

"What did he say?"

"You don't want to know."

I followed Clemson through the underbrush. Duke met us at the edge of the staff camp. When he saw Clemson, he burst into dialect and pointed at me.

"All right," Clemson said. "Where is it?"

"Let me get my bearings."

I wondered around the camp, looking at the tents. Found the one with the half-rolled flap. I went around to the back, sighted a perpendicular to the back wall, and paced off ten yards into the bush.

The stick wasn't there.

That was okay. Ten yards was an approximation. So was my perpendicular. It was not necessarily a right angle, nor had I necessarily walked one.

"Where is it?" Clemson said.

"It's here. On the ground. In this area."

I paced off a ten-foot square on the

ground in the heart of where the club must lie.

"There. It's a large stick with blood on it. We just have to look around until we find it."

We looked around, but we didn't find it. The stick was not there.

17
WEAPONLESS

I was beginning to feel like the hero in one of those exasperating movies where he knows something is wrong but no one will believe him. There's a zillion of them, ranging all the way from the most dreadful low-budget horror movie right up to classics like *Rear Window*. Unfortunately, I wasn't Jimmy Stewart. I was a B-movie actor, only slightly less popular than pond scum.

"So you're the one spreading the rumor," the other husband said in a peevish way as we gathered before dinner.

"What rumor?"

"That it wasn't an accident. That someone killed the boy."

It was clear enough what he meant from his tone. He might as well have said, *so you're the troublemaker.*

The afternoon hike had been changed to a game drive. Due to my allegations, Duke had spent the afternoon questioning the staff, leaving John's group with no ranger. Clemson canceled the hikes, gave Mowangi's ranger the afternoon off, and sent out the jeeps with guides and spotters.

We probably saw something, but whatever it was wasn't memorable enough to leave an impression. I was too wrapped up in my thoughts. Discovering the stick strongly pointed to foul play. The fact that it was missing clinched it. At least to my satisfaction. As far as anyone else was concerned, I was either making it up or had imagined it.

"It's not a rumor and I'm not spreading it," I said. "I found a bloody stick. Duke's checking it out."

"It seems a waste of time. What's he expect to find?"

"I doubt if he expects to find anything, but it's his job."

Keith and the other man came over. "You really think it's a murder?"

"I wouldn't go that far. I really think Daniel was hit with a stick, not a sausage fruit."

"Which would be murder."

"It could be self-defense."

"If it was self-defense, why wouldn't someone say so?"

"Self-defense isn't that easy to prove. Between pleading self-defense and hoping people think he got hit with a sausage fruit,

138

I'd go with the fruit every time."

"That's stupid," Keith said.

It was just us boys hanging out. The four of us were all the men there were in the party. The other seven tourists were all women. Which was fine with me. It was just if the killer was one of us, there were only four male suspects. That's no knock at women, who make absolutely dandy killers. But hitting someone over the head with a club seemed a manly thing to do.

If a woman *had* killed Daniel, my first choice for a candidate, Hells Angel #2, came barging up saying, "You guys picking on Stanley?"

They were, but I wasn't sure I wanted to be defended by a Hells Angel, amorous or not. "They're taking their justly deserved shots," I said. "If you want to join them, fire away."

"Wouldn't dream of it," she said, then proceeded to do so. "Who in the world would want to kill a nice young boy like that? It makes no sense. An accident I could understand. But a murder? That's really stretching it, don't you think?"

I didn't think, but I wasn't about to argue.

Lolita's mother came next, predictably seeing this all as an attack on her and her daughter. "If this is true, how are any of us safe? Did you think about that before you made these wild accusations?"

I could honestly say that I had not weighed the impact on the safety of the group before I made my accusations. At least it had never occurred to me it might affect them in a negative way. Exposing a killer, it seemed to me, would be doing just the opposite.

Alice 2, the one I wasn't married to, joined the discussion. "This is silly. Going around questioning the staff. It would make more sense to question us."

Lolita's mother's mouth dropped open. "But we don't know anything," she protested.

Alice 2 smiled. "We may *think* we don't. But we may know something and not know that we know it. I've been reading Agatha Christie novels, and I must say they're very good. And the main clue in the story is usually given by someone who doesn't know that what they know is important. Some minor detail, like Daniel's searchlight."

The other husband said, "What about his searchlight?"

"That was just an example. A bad one, I admit, and I don't have a good one. If I did, I'd know why it was a good one. I'd know why it was important. I'd know what it meant."

Hells Angel #1 showed up for the end of that conversation. "Know what what meant?"

"A clue to what happened," Keith said.

"You have a clue to what happened?"

"No," Alice 2 said. "I'm just saying if I did, I might not know it was important. Still, it might come out through careful questioning."

Alice and Lolita showed up chatting. That couldn't be good. I wondered what they were talking about. I hoped it wasn't me.

"Well, what's everyone talking about?" Alice said.

"As if we didn't know," Lolita said. She looked at me with a malicious twinkle. "You didn't say you were a private investigator. Can you believe that? An actual PI."

"You're a PI?" Alice 2 said, which set off a round of my I'm-not-that-type-of-detective-I-just-chase-ambulances routine.

No one was buying it. As far as they were concerned, I fancied myself some hotshot TV detective, which was why I was spoiling their fun by mistaking this unfortunate accident for a murder.

The other wife joined us, completing the party. She had just come from her tent so she had no idea what was going on, but she sensed the tension.

"What's the matter?" she said.

Her husband pointed to me. "He's a PI."

"What?"

"He's a private investigator," Lolita said. "He's going to solve Daniel's murder."

I wished she hadn't said that, and with such a wicked twinkle in her eye. It was like she was deliberately setting me up again.

The wife stared at me. "You're a detective?"

"Not a police detective," I said. "I handle negligence claims."

"Negligence? What has that got to do with Daniel?"

"It doesn't. I stumbled on the stick that killed him. Quite by accident. Duke's looking into it. It's his job."

"Phooey," Alice 2 said. "You think he's going to find anything? He couldn't even find the stick."

"That's hardly his fault. I couldn't find it either. Somebody took the stick."

"So you say," Keith said.

I wasn't going to rise to that bait. I was willing to let the implication lie.

Alice 2 wasn't. "What do you mean by that?" she said. "Are you accusing him of lying?"

"No," Keith said. "I'm sure he *thinks* he found the stick."

I would have preferred an accusation. His patronizing condescension was more annoying and harder to deal with. Not that I was about to.

Unfortunately, I had a protector.

"Don't be silly," Alice 2 said. "Stanley's a private investigator. You think he doesn't know a murder weapon when he sees one?"

"Oh, sure," Keith said. "Are you telling me you can tell the difference between a stick that killed someone and a stick a farmer used to kill a pig?"

"Absolutely not," I said. "I don't have that type of training, that type of expertise."

I hoped that admission would make me sound amateurish enough not to be considered a serious threat to be solving any murders.

Unfortunately, it had the reverse effect. Television was awash with self-deprecating macho PIs. Pooh-poohing my abilities was obviously a clear indication of how confident I was in them.

"So," Alice 2 said. "Assuming the killer's one of us, are you going to question us all to see if anyone makes a slip?"

"Is that what they do in the books you read?"

She cocked her head at me. "I'm sure you read them too."

"Of course I do. But I know the difference between fiction and real life."

"I'm not really interested in a philosophical discussion about books," the other husband said. "The point is, are you going to go around interrogating people about a murder?"

I took a breath. "As I said before, that's not my job."

"I know it's not your job. I'm asking if you intend to do it."

"No, I do not."

"Oh, don't get all huffy on us just because some people questioned your authority," Alice 2 said. "If anyone's going to make an independent investigation, it ought to be you. You're the only one with experience."

Clemson came walking up for the tail end of that. "Experience with what?" he said.

"Crime," Alice 2 said. She pointed at me triumphantly. "Stanley's a private investigator."

Clemson looked at me with what, were I not a tourist, would have been distaste. "Oh, is he really?" he said dryly.

18
Bush Shower

Dinner that night was subdued. People just sat and packed it in. We had salad, meat, mashed potatoes, and some sort of vegetable. I had no idea what it was, nor had I any idea what was in the salad. I just knew it had a lot of greens, and the dressing wasn't much. Alice, to her credit, didn't complain, as she usually does in the absence of balsamic vinaigrette, but she like the rest of us was restrained.

The meat might have been chicken, beef, or warthog. I barely tasted it. I kept looking around at my fellow travelers, wondering which of them might be a killer. I didn't think any of them were, but Alice 2 had made me suspicious, just as she had made everyone suspicious. The number of surreptitious sidelong glances escalated geometrically as we sized each other up, trying to decide if we were killers, victims, or sleuths. I was doing it myself, even though I was sure I knew the answer. We were none of the above. The victim was Zambian. The killer was Zambian. The detective investigating the crime, Duke, was Zambian. We were a group of tourists unlucky enough to have barely known the victim, an employee, hired to assist the employees hired by Clemson to assist us. Sort of like a second cousin twice removed, whatever the hell that means. I've never understood the expression, though it always conjured up the image of some secret society of terrorists who went around removing cousins.

I was not so distracted by my thoughts as not to notice Alice 2 managing to chat with various guests. She would get up, take her plate to the buffet, if one can use the term for a single folding table, make a show of adding some salad or vegetable to her plate, position herself next to someone else, and make a token show of eating it. Once I picked up on this behavior, I began clocking her movements. She spoke to Lolita, and she spoke to Lolita's mother, each separately. It couldn't have been easy. I wondered what she was asking them. I would have asked her, if she ever spoke to me, but she didn't. I guess she figured I was the detective and above suspicion. Which wasn't really logical if she was a murder mystery buff, where the detective as the surprise killer was always an option.

At any rate, those were the only two I saw her question. She skipped me and Alice, which made four. She was the fifth. That left six members of our party, Keith and his traveling companion, the husband and wife, and the two Hells Angels. I don't know which of those, if any, she questioned before I took notice. Another question I was going to ask her if she came over.

But she didn't. She skipped dessert, some sort of runny pudding I also passed on after an initial bite. I stepped up to the table to trade in my full bowl for a cup of coffee, and when I turned around she was gone.

I suddenly had a wild premonition I would never see her again, that she would be the member of the party that disappears, stolen away in the night by a marauding band of second-cousin removers.

I confided my fears to Alice once we were back in the confines of our tent, knowing that she would ground me in reality.

"You're wrong," Alice said, which put things in their true perspective. It was a simple situation and I was reading too much into it.

It took me a few moments to notice the discrepancy. "But you told me to investigate.

This afternoon. Right in this very tent. You told me I had to look into it."

"No, I didn't."

"Come on. We had the whole discussion about the sausage fruit and the blow to the back of his head. I said the sausage fruit couldn't have caused it, and you said I had to investigate."

"I didn't say you had to."

"I beg to differ."

"Feel free."

"You said it had to be investigated."

"Yes."

"And I told you Duke wasn't going to do it."

"Yes."

"You weren't happy with that answer, were you?"

"No."

"So I had to investigate."

"Ah. You volunteered your services. I thought so."

"And then you had to go tell people I was a private investigator." I said "people" so I wouldn't have to say "the hot teenage chick whose tits I saw through the mosquito netting peep show."

"You *are* a private investigator."

"You didn't have to say so."

"You want me to call you a writer? My

148

husband's a famous screenwriter. Did the screenplay for the Jason Clairemont kung fu movie, *Hands of Havoc, Flesh of Fire.*"

"Alice —"

"I think it's great that you found the murder weapon. Now Duke's investigating. The odds that it's one of us are rather poor. That's good. It means he's investigating the right people. If it weren't for Alice talking about murder mysteries, you'd think so too."

It was strange hearing Alice talk about Alice. I was trapped between two Alices. The voice of reason, and the voice of mystery fiction.

"Come on," Alice said. "I want to take a shower."

"Great."

"Not together."

"You said come on."

"You can take one after me. Put the side flaps down."

"Huh?"

"We're getting undressed. You want to give the other campers a thrill? Put the flaps down."

I went out of the tent, unrolled the side flaps. Some of the ties were snarled, so it wasn't easy. By the time I got back inside, Alice was wearing a bath towel.

"No fair," I said. "You send me out and

then change."

"Don't be juvenile. Come on, get ready."

I pulled off my safari outfit, wrapped a bath towel around my waist.

Alice was wearing one of the little headband flashlights. She handed me mine. "Here."

I put it on my forehead. "I feel like a miner."

"Just don't lose it. Come on, let's go."

The shower stall was a good twenty yards off to the side of the straight-drop toilet. It was a canvas structure quite like it, only taller. Instead of a hole in the ground, it had a slatted wooden platform. There was no running water, of course. Hot water was poured into a bag connected to a shower-head that hung just out of reach. You paraded to the shower in the threadbare towels provided by the camp, and, often as not, stood outside waiting your turn, since our schedule led to all of us needing to shower more or less at the same time, generally before or after dinner. No one showered before or after breakfast. You woke up and hit the road.

Alice and I got lucky. There was someone in the shower, but no line. As we walked up, there came the sound of the water being shut off.

"Well, that's a stroke of luck," Alice said.

It was indeed. Moments later Lolita popped out, clad in a skimpy towel.

"Good timing," she said. "They just filled the bag." She smiled mischievously. "Have fun!"

"Yeah, right," Alice said. "I'll go first."

"Want me to turn on the water for you?" I offered.

"I'll manage," Alice said, and slipped through the canvas flap.

"Too bad," Lolita said. "It's more fun to shower with a pal."

Lolita's towel was slipping. She untucked it, straightened it, retucked it. The move was incredibly erotic. It wasn't revealing, just an amazing tease. The dance of the seven veils reimagined as the dance of the one frayed bath towel.

I felt a rustling in my frayed bath towel unbecoming in a middle-aged married man.

Hells Angel #2 walked up, bursting her bath towel, just as Lolita left.

"Someone's in there?" she said.

"My wife."

"Ah. And you're a gentleman, letting her go first."

"Actually, I tried to pile in there with her. She was having none of it."

Her eyes twinkled. "Naughty boy."

151

The water shut off and Alice came out. "You probably better wait," she said. "The water's almost gone."

"Oh, great."

"Don't worry. They'll come fill it up. They know one bag's not enough for the whole camp. Oh, here they are now."

Two of the staff emerged from the darkness, carrying the heavy bucket. I couldn't recognize either of them. Which was awful. I'd seen them around camp, I just couldn't distinguish one from another. They didn't have any single function to identify them. Like a guide or a spotter or an apprentice. They didn't look happy. I wondered if Duke had been interrogating them all afternoon.

They untied a rope, lowered the bag with showerhead attached, filled it from the bucket, and pulled it back up again. The whole operation took less than a minute. They nodded, flashing a good deal of pearly teeth, and disappeared into the darkness. So much for the irritated and cranky theory. They were just straining from the weight of the water.

For a moment I wondered if I should be a gentleman and let Hells Angel #2 go first. A brief moment. If I did, more women would show up and I'd wind up standing there all night.

"Here goes," I said.

"Save me some water," she said.

"Don't worry, I'll be quick."

I slipped inside, took off my towel, hung it on the nail provided. I reached up, turned the water on. Just in time, I remembered the headlight. I hung it on the nail with my towel, and stepped under the shower. The flow was erratic, but the water was hot. I grabbed a bar of soap, lathered up my armpits and nether regions, and twirled around in the spray, rinsing the soapsuds off. I didn't wash my hair, just wet it. It wasn't much of a shower. I probably broke the record of Speedy Gonzalez.

I'd like to think I was being considerate and saving water. If the truth be known, I was also trying to get out of there before an amorous Hells Angel ripped the canvas aside and climbed in with me. Anyway, I hadn't used much water and I figured she'd be grateful.

I'm not sure she noticed. When I came out, she was deep in conversation with Keith. The young man was looking boyishly slim in his bath towel. I must say I resented every rippled muscle. The only consolation was, for Keith maturity surely would be a bitter disappointment.

I switched on my headlight, made my way

back to my tent.

Alice, of course, was completely dried off and ready for bed. Her bed.

I dropped my towel on the ground.

"Stanley!"

"What?"

"Must you?"

"Must I what?"

"Put your clothes on. You're making a spectacle of yourself."

"Glad you noticed."

"Good thing the tent flaps are down. You'd be the talk of breakfast."

"You think I'm that spectacular?"

"I think you're that ridiculous. Why are you so sexed up? Did Victoria hit on you?"

"Victoria?"

"Yes. Her name's Victoria. Her sister's name is Annabel. Was she flirting with you?"

"Victoria's the young, horny one?"

"Can't you tell?"

"Alice, I'm an old noncom. I'm lucky if I can guess a woman's age within twenty years."

"Oh, for goodness sakes. Yes, she's the nymphomaniac. If she wasn't hitting on you, you're even older than you think."

"I'm much older than I think. No, she wasn't. I think she has a crush on Keith."

"How could she *not* have a crush on

Keith? He's young and good-looking, Stanley."

I pulled on the T-shirt I sleep in and lay down in bed. I was not a happy camper. I was the oldest man on the planet. No one found me attractive.

Not even Victoria, the amorous Hells Angel.

19
OVERSLEPT

Alice 2 wasn't at breakfast. It took a while to notice because everyone drifted in. It began, as usual, with the sight of John and Mowangi grilling toast over the campfires while an assortment of murder suspects came and went, loading the buffet table with plates of food from wherever they were cooking it.

I couldn't eat a thing, but did, actually chewed my way through two large slabs of toast. I washed it down with particularly bitter coffee. I put sugar in it, something I never do. It immediately dissolved. No surprise there. It was a wonder it didn't dissolve the spoon.

Alice was up early. Alice 1, my Alice, the Alice of my eye. She couldn't sleep, per usual, was up and out and greeting the dawn before I knew there was any dawn to greet.

She wasn't the first to breakfast, however.

When we wandered over, the other married couple was already there. I still didn't know their names, and I wasn't about to learn them, because no one brought their water bottles to breakfast. The easy way would be to ask them, but at this phase of the trip not to know their names would be insulting. I figured the only thing to do was bluff it through until I stumbled on their names by accident.

The Hells Angels wandered in right after me. I knew their names now. Victoria and Annabel. Keith walked in shortly after that with his traveling companion to be named later, followed by the other two women in the party. I didn't know their names either, but it didn't matter. To me they would always be Lolita and her mother.

Alice was conferring with Clemson. I think it had something to do with camera settings. I tuned right out, considered having another piece of toast. I wasn't about to risk whatever the other slop they were dishing out was. Not in my delicate Malarone condition.

Hells Angel #2 sat down next to me. I realized I knew her name. Before I could use it, she spotted Keith, bounced up and skittered on amorous Hells Angel feet across the campsite to continue the conversation they'd been having the night before. Assuming they hadn't hooked up in the meantime. She didn't seem like Keith's type, but then I didn't know what Keith's type was. Yes, I did. Lolita.

Alice dropped into the chair next to me long enough to stash her backpack and admonish me to keep an eye on it, a lose-lose proposition. In addition to being responsible for the whereabouts of the backpack, I was now responsible for its contents, as in, "Are the tissues in my backpack?" "I have no idea." "Well, you had it." And off she went to the buffet table, inspecting every last item as if she had a cast-iron stomach. She in fact does not, though she was reacting to the Malarone far better than I.

Breakfast progressed. Food was consumed, conversation resumed. It all related to the events of the coming day. There was no talk of the death of Daniel.

By the end of breakfast, Alice had drifted off god knows where, and I was sweating out the guardianship of the backpack. Should I sit here and mind it until she came back, or did I assume she had gone to the tent and take it there? If I went to the tent, Alice would demand to know why I'd abandoned my post at the campfire. And if I stayed at my appointed spot, Alice would demand to know if I was a moron who intended to stay there all day.

While this was going on, I noticed Clemson summon one of the breakfast-cooking, hot-water-for-showers-toting staff men over and engage in a whispered conversation, whereupon the young man took off in the direction of the tourists' tents.

To increase my dilemma, Clemson announced that the walks would be taking off in ten minutes. I wasn't walking anywhere without consulting the straight-drop toilet, in my opinion the ultimate authority on hiking. I glanced covetously in its direction and saw Alice returning from it. Excellent. I waved to her, but she veered off in the direction of our tent.

It was too much. Alice was going to stay in the tent until the last minute, and when she came back I'd have to run off to the straight-drop toilet and hold up the hike. And Alice would blame me for it.

As I sat there in helpless frustration, Hells Angel #2 brought her backpack and sat down next to me. Under the circumstances Alice wouldn't hold it against me if I passed the buck. Surely I could ask Hells Angel #2 for a favor. It would be easy since I knew her name.

I looked over at her. "Victoria?"

She didn't respond.

I raised my voice. "Victoria?"

She looked. "Were you talking to me?"

"Yes."

"My name's not Victoria."

I blinked. Wrong again. "Oh," I said. "That's your sister."

"My sister?"

"Yes. Your sister's Victoria."

"I haven't got a sister."

"The woman you're traveling with. She's not your sister?"

She laughed. "Goodness, no. We barely know each other. We're librarians. Met on Dorothyl."

"Dorothy El?"

"It's a list-serve. For mystery readers."

"List-serve?"

She laughed. "You don't use the computer much. Dorothyl is an on-line discussion group named after Dorothy L. Sayers. You know who that is?"

"Did she write *The Daughter of Time*?"

"That's Josephine Tey. But you're in the ballpark. Anyway, we met online discussing Lawrence Block. He had a new Burglar book out after years, and we're both huge fans. Anyway, she mentioned going to Zambia and her husband doesn't travel and it turns out it's much more expensive if you go as a single. My husband's not much of a traveler either, and —"

She kept rambling on, but I barely heard. My head was spinning.

The Hells Angels weren't sisters. And they weren't Hells Angels. They were married librarians. And they weren't named Victoria and Annabel. The woman was talking to me, and I still didn't know who she was. I just knew who she wasn't.

So if the Hells Angels weren't the sisters named Victoria and Annabel, who were? The only other women in the party were Alice 2, who was traveling alone, the woman who was traveling with her husband, and Lolita and her mother.

My eyes widened. My stomach felt hollow as layer after layer of reality slipped out from under me.

Lolita and her mother?

At that moment, the staff man ran up jabbering hysterically in dialect and pointing toward the tents.

Clemson sprang up and ran off in that direction.

I was right on his heels.

I was halfway to the tents before I realized I'd abandoned my backpack.

I kept going.

Clemson and the staff man reached a tent.

The staff man lifted the flap and Clemson ducked inside.

I tried to follow, but the staff man put up his hand. I didn't push by him, but I didn't back up either. I stood my ground, looked around him.

Alice 2 was lying on her cot. Clemson was trying to rouse her.

From her glassy-eyed stare and the froth on her lips, I could tell he wasn't going to have any luck.

20
MURDER?

"She died in her sleep."

"I'm sure you'd like to think that."

"I think that," Clemson said, "because that's what she did. She went to bed and she didn't wake up."

"How do you know? Are you a doctor?"

"It doesn't take a doctor to know she's dead."

"It takes a doctor to know why. Did you see the saliva on her chin? That doesn't look like she died peacefully in her sleep. That looks like she was poisoned."

"If that's the case, the doctor will determine it."

"What doctor?"

"The doctor at the U.S. Embassy in Lusaka."

"You sent the body to the U.S. Embassy?"

"I have to. When an American tourist dies on safari, the consulate steps in."

"What if it turns out she was poisoned?"

"It will make a huge difference *how* she was poisoned. If she was given arsenic, that's one thing. If she ate a poison plant, that's another. A poison plant could be accidental."

"I fail to see how."

"I understand she ate a lot last night. If a plant got in her salad."

"How would a plant get in her salad?"

"I have no idea."

Clemson was sitting in a chair by the campfire, drinking a Coke Lite. I had declined the offer of one and was standing. The rest of the tourists had gone out. The death of Alice 2 was certainly sad, but no one came to Africa to go into mourning. Not considering the price of airfare. The morning walk wasn't canceled. It went out late, and it was changed to a game drive, but it went out.

Duke was questioning the staff again, which seemed an empty gesture. If anyone had killed Alice 2, it was us.

"Did you hear what she was saying at dinner?" I said.

"I did not hear what she was saying at dinner. I heard what you *said* she was saying at dinner."

"Are you deliberately being annoying?"

"Not at all. I stayed back from the game

drive because I have to. I'm in charge. You, on the other hand, should by all rights be bumping along in a jeep looking for lions."

"Give me a break. Daniel's killed. Alice 2 starts shooting her mouth off about how one of us must have done it."

"Alice 2?"

"I don't know her last name. The Alice I'm not married to. The dead woman. She was saying one of us must have done it. Moreover, she was saying some of us must know something that would shed some light on who did it. If the killer heard that, and the killer thought she was right, then the killer would know she had to go."

"So he fed her a lethal dose of poison plants?"

"Or slipped her arsenic. The poison plants are your idea."

"The whole idea of poison is yours," Clemson said.

"Based on the physical evidence."

"Based on *your interpretation* of the physical evidence. Pardon me if I missed something, but I don't believe you're that type of detective, are you?"

"Not at all. But I've been at a lot of crime scenes. I've seen enough dead bodies I don't even throw up any more."

Clemson looked at me with distaste. "I

have not seen a lot of dead bodies. We hadn't had many until you showed up."

"What are you implying?"

"I'm not implying anything."

"If you're implying I'm the killer, you're admitting there's a killer."

"I think you're having too much fun with this."

"I'm not having fun with this. You know how many vacations I've had in my life? One. This one. Alice and I have never taken a trip out of the country before. This is not how I expected to spend it."

"Then you better be damn careful with your accusations of murder. If this is a murder, your trip is toast. How'd you like to be hauled into the embassy and grilled as suspects?"

"My wife would never forgive me."

"There you are."

"Is Duke going to question the tourists?"

"He's not equipped to do so."

"Are you?"

"I'm not in a position to do so either."

"I see."

"That doesn't mean you should."

"That doesn't mean I shouldn't."

Clemson frowned. "If you want to ask questions, I can't stop you. But if you could refrain from spreading rumors."

"Like the rumors about Daniel?"

"There's no proof he was killed either."

"And yet Duke is investigating."

"On your say-so. Which is the same reason Alice was investigating."

"You concede she was?"

"Concede?" Clemson made a face. "Must you treat this like a game? The woman died. We're investigating because we have to. But that doesn't mean we think that she was killed."

For my money, he was trying awfully hard to sound like he believed it.

21
Go Ask Alice

"Well, what did he say?" Alice demanded.

"Hi, hello, how are you, how was your drive?" I said.

"Don't be a jerk. Did you have any luck with Clemson?"

"Not a lot. Clemson doesn't think she was murdered. If she was, he thinks I did it."

Alice groaned. "Oh, for goodness sakes. What did you say to deserve that?"

"It's not my fault. I was polite."

"Dealing with strangers polite, or the way you talk to MacAullif?"

Sergeant MacAullif was the police officer with whom I'd dealt in a number of homicides. Polite conversation with him consisted of hurling sarcastic vulgarities at each other.

"I was on my best behavior. If he took offense, he's thin-skinned." Alice was thoroughly dissatisfied with that answer. I quickly changed the subject. "What about you?"

"What do you mean?"

"Did you question people?"

"I'm not the detective."

"You're very perceptive. You have good instincts."

"What do you want?"

"What do you mean?"

"Your whole toadying routine. You start flattering me, you must want something."

What I wanted was for Alice to stop assessing my performance with Clemson, and I'm pretty sure she knew it. I wondered if she was beating me up for practice. But I wasn't about to say *that.*

"Come on, Alice, it must have been the topic of conversation. What happened on the game drive?"

"Oh. Well, I was in Mowangi's group. That was the larger party."

"Six?"

"Five. We didn't have you. John's group was four. He didn't have Clemson or Alice. We had Victoria and Annabel and Keith and Jason."

"Jason?"

"The man traveling with Keith."

By process of elimination I had come to the realization that Victoria and Annabel were the sisters formerly known as Lolita and Lolita's mother. How long it would take me to live down that ignominy I had no idea. Luckily, Alice didn't know that was how I designated them. She just thought I was too dumb to know which was the young sexy one. I'm just glad she didn't know how *well* I knew which was the young sexy one.

"And what did they say?" I ventured non-committally.

"It was hard to talk to Annabel and Victoria together. Annabel has to be constantly vigilant Victoria's not making a spectacle of herself. Even you must have noticed how nervous she is."

"I have. I just didn't know it was that."

"Please. The woman's a nervous wreck. Anyway, the drive was particularly strained because Victoria and Keith were together. I don't mean together, but in the same group. So I had to deal with that on top of the Alice situation."

"Oh, dear."

"What?"

"Has it come to that? Are we really referring to it as the Alice situation?"

"Well, you haven't determined it's a murder yet, have you?"

"It's not my job. Clemson's waiting for the medical report."

"Will there be one?"

"So he says. When it's an American tourist the consulate gets touchy."

"Well no one thinks it's a murder except Annabel, who's scared of shadows. Victoria thinks it's silly. So do Keith and Jason."

"What do they think happened?"

"She died in her sleep. Or accidently ate a poison plant."

"That's Clemson's idea too."

"Really?"

"If it was poison. And he's not conceding it is. What else did you get?"

"What do you mean?"

"Who was close to her?"

"Well, none of them. They weren't really her type."

"What's her type?"

"She was older. She read murder mysteries."

"The librarians read murder mysteries."

"What?"

"The other women traveling together. They're librarians, and they read murder mysteries and discuss 'em on the Internet."

"Do people really do that?"

"Apparently."

"Some people have way too much time on their hands."

"Yeah. I didn't really mean were they in her circle of acquaintances. She thought there was something suspicious about Daniel's death. She mentioned asking people about it. I was wondering if she did. Did she talk to any of them?"

"They all say no."

"That's interesting."

"Why?"

"Well, we know she talked to someone."

"How do we know that?"

"Because she's dead."

"So that's your theory."

"Isn't it obvious?"

"Yes."

It's amazing how she does that. Manages to contradict me with a single syllable. She does it by agreeing with me. When Alice agrees with me, something's wrong. If Alice agreed with me, it was time to reevaluate my entire position.

In this case it was easy. The idea that Alice 2 was killed for poking into Daniel's death was obvious.

That didn't make it true.

22
QUESTIONS

I had a problem at lunch. My problem was I wanted to question people about Alice 2. But if I questioned the ones Alice had already questioned, it would seem like I didn't trust her judgment. The number of good husband points that might cost me was incalculable. Still, I couldn't compromise a murder investigation for the sake of my own wellbeing. Alice would be mad if I did. So there I was, once again, caught in a no-win situation. My default position.

I sidled up to Hells Angel #2, said, "Hey, babe, how's it going?"

She looked at me to see if I'd taken leave of my senses, caught the twinkle in my eye. "It isn't going well, that's for sure. Except to the game drive. We actually saw a lion."

"Really?"

"He ran away."

"So you have no photographic evidence."

"I'm afraid not. You'll have to take my

word for it."

"Among other things."

"Huh?"

"Were people talking about Alice?"

"Of course."

"What is the general consensus?"

"She died in her sleep."

"Really?"

"You think she was killed?"

"Do you?"

"I have no idea."

"Well, that's not exactly true, is it?" I said.

"I beg your pardon?"

"Come, come. You read murder mysteries and discuss them on the Internet. You have a friend who does the same thing. Surely you've discussed the possibility."

"Well, we've discussed it, but that doesn't mean we believe it. Right, Edith?"

Hells Angel #1 sat down with us. "Doesn't mean we believe what?"

"It doesn't mean we think Alice was killed. Yeah, we read murder mysteries. So what? So did she."

"And that's significant," I said.

Hells Angel #1, who I now knew to be Edith, looked at me. "Are you saying you think we're in danger?"

"I think we should all be on our guard. But that's not what I meant. Last night Alice talked about murder investigations, and questioning people, and people with clues who knew something they didn't even know was important. She even mentioned Agatha Christie."

"So?"

"Neither one of you jumped in."

They looked at each other.

Edith said, "She was talking about that poor boy's death as if it were a game. As if it were just for our amusement. We'd have felt uncomfortable joining in."

I frowned.

Edith said, "You can't understand that?"

"People aren't always that nice."

"They should be."

"Yes, they should. Tell me, do you have the same scruples regarding Alice's murder?"

"You think it's a murder?"

"Don't you?"

"It's a little different," Edith said. "You have a young boy who never hurt anyone. And then you have a woman on a murder hunt."

"You think she was killed because of it?"

"I have no idea."

"But you grant the possibility?"

"Of course."

"Then you have to concede the possibility

175

Daniel's death was a murder. Investigating Daniel's murder wouldn't scare anyone if there's no murderer."

"Oh, I don't know about that," Edith said.

"Why not?"

"Suppose someone has something *else* to hide? She pokes around and comes up with it. It has nothing to do with the death of that young boy. But if it's something someone doesn't want revealed, they might kill to cover it up."

I was impressed. That was a more logical line of reasoning than I'd come up with. I suddenly realized that that was what Alice meant when she undermined my confidence by agreeing with me. "You have any idea what that might be?"

"Of course not."

"What about the couple you were out with this morning? Did you talk to them?"

"Of course we talked to them," Hells Angel #2 said. I wished Edith would address her by name. "It would be rude to ignore them."

"And?"

"What?"

I realized it was like talking to Alice. "And what did they say about Alice's murder?"

"No one said it was a murder."

"Alice's death."

176

"They weren't concerned. They figured she died in her sleep."

"They were a little concerned," Hells Angel #2 amended. "Simon asked —"

"His name is Simon?"

"Of course."

"And her name?"

"Her name is Trish. Simon and Trish."

"And Trish wasn't concerned but Simon was?"

"He was jumpy. Nervous. But I'm sure it wasn't about that."

"If you ask me," Edith said, "the one who was really bothered by her death was Mowangi."

"Mowangi?" I said. "Why do you say that?"

"I don't know. But he was a little off his game. Like I asked what some bird was and he hadn't seen it."

"So he missed some bird or other."

"But he's *always* seen it. He prides himself on seeing it. Haven't you noticed that?"

"We usually went with John."

"Well, if you ask me who's taking it hardest, it's him."

"Fine," I said. "But the guy —" I groped for the name. "Simon. You said he was jumpy?"

"Yes. But he always seems a little jumpy."

That was interesting. I waited until Simon got up to get something from the buffet table, and walked over and sat in his spot.

Trish was surprised to see me. "Ah, my husband's sitting there."

"Yeah, right," I said. I made no attempt to get up. "Tell me about the morning drive."

She blinked. "What about it?"

"Clemson and I missed it. I'm wondering how it was."

"Nothing special."

"Really. One of us just died. Or didn't you notice?"

"I thought you meant what we saw. And it was nothing special."

Simon returned with a plate of food. Saw me sitting there. Stopped. Cleared his throat. "Excuse me. I was sitting there."

"Yes," I said. "I was just talking to Trish about the morning drive. She says it was nothing special."

"Well, it wasn't."

"Yeah. As I pointed out to Trish, there weren't many of us on it. Your jeep only had four people."

"Look, that's my seat."

"You were kind of nervous on the morning drive. Was that because someone had been killed?"

"No one was killed. An old lady died in

her sleep."

"She wasn't that old."

"Old enough. You can't live forever."

"What were you so worried about?"

"I wasn't worried!" Simon almost shouted it. "Why are you asking so many questions? First her, then you."

"Her?"

He looked flustered. After a moment, he said, "My wife asks a lot of questions."

"I wasn't asking questions," Trish protested.

"I didn't say you *were* asking a lot of questions. I said you *do* ask a lot of questions. Which is a good thing. It's how you learn. What would be the point of coming all this way if we didn't learn?"

"What did Alice ask you?"

"Nothing. She didn't ask me anything."

"How about you, Trish?"

"The whole idea was upsetting. I didn't speak to her."

"At all?"

"No. I went back to my tent after dinner."

"And you?"

Simon took a breath. "I resent you asking these questions. And you're sitting in my seat."

"Oh. Why didn't you say so?"

I got up and walked away, leaving him

standing there with egg on his face.

Lolita/Victoria grabbed my arm and pulled me aside. Her mother/sister wasn't around.

Neither was Alice. Talking to the girl outside of her presence was most likely a disaster of epic proportions. But I was conducting a murder investigation. And *she* was the one who pulled *me* aside. Though there wasn't a woman alive on the planet would be satisfied with the well-she-wanted-it defense.

"You have to help me," she said. "You're the only one I can trust."

Oh, god. Kill me now.

"What's the matter?"

"It's my sister."

"What about her?"

"You must have noticed. She has problems."

Of which you're the biggest one, was the phrase that came to mind. I did not voice it.

"She's very neurotic. Very fearful. She imagines things."

"Like what?"

"She thinks someone's trying to kill her."

"If it turns out Alice was killed, that's not necessarily neurotic."

"Yes, yes," she said impatiently. "Just

because you're paranoid doesn't mean they're not out to get you. That's not the *only* thing that worries her. At the moment it's uppermost in her mind."

"What do you expect me to do?"

She clung to my arm, looked up into my eyes. The effect was disconcerting. "You're the detective. You're the only one who knows what's going on here. You're the only one with any chance of figuring it out. Basically, you're our only hope."

"You want me to solve the crime so your sister won't be nervous?"

"You make it sound ridiculous."

"Well, you say it so it's not ridiculous."

"I saw you questioning everybody, trying to find out what happened."

"So?"

"Take it easy on her. If you push her too hard, she'll break. Then where will we be?"

"Relax. I'm not going to hound your sister."

"You may not think so. What you think are casual questions she may take as an interrogation."

"I think you're exaggerating a little."

"You don't know her. She has crazy ideas."

"If she's so hard to get along with, why do you travel with her?"

She made a face. "She's my older sister.

She controls the money."

"Until you're of age."

"Please. I'm twenty-six. She's thirty-five. She came into her money. I don't come into mine until I'm thirty-five. Till then, I have a trustee."

"Don't tell me."

"That's right. We had the same trustee until she reached maturity. At which time she became mine. I can afford to travel with her. I can't afford to travel alone."

"And I assume there's no way to break the trust?"

"Not according to Fitzhugh, Rozan, and Billheimer. Or Phillips, Brewer and Burcell. The trust is judgment-proof. Even Randisi and Stilwell won't touch it."

"Poor little rich girl."

"Yes. So that's why I'm traveling with her even though it's not easy. But don't get the wrong idea. Just because she's difficult doesn't mean I don't like her. I don't want anything to happen to her, and I don't trust her to take care of herself."

She pulled me closer, looked up into my eyes and said earnestly, "Can I count on you?"

Out of the corner of my eye, I could see Alice bearing down on us just in time to see her clinging to me like a vine.

"Of course," I said.

23
BAD BOY

"What did I tell you?"

"I know what you told me, Alice."

"I leave you alone for five minutes, you're making a play for a nymphomaniac."

"She's not a nymphomaniac."

"Yeah, right."

"She's not promiscuous. She's just uninhibited. She's worried about her sister."

"Of course she is. Her sister's trying to squelch her action."

"You don't understand."

"Stanley, it's a relationship thing. You've not good with relationship things."

"And yet our marriage endures."

"Don't be an idiot."

"Alice, it's not what you think. According to her, her sister's emotionally disturbed."

"You think that's news? A child of four can see she's emotionally disturbed. It doesn't alter the fact her sister's a nymphomaniac."

"That's what her sister claims. If the sister's not right in the head —"

"Stanley, she was climbing all over you."

"She was upset."

"She was horny."

"If she was horny, she'd be making a play for Keith."

"She *is* making a play for Keith."

"Oh?"

"She was trying to flirt with him all morning. Her sister kept interfering."

"You didn't mention that."

"I'm sorry. Didn't I get my priorities straight? I thought you were interested in the murder."

"I'm interested in the motivations of the suspects."

"And one in particular."

"You're just upset because I'm interviewing the same people you talked to."

"Oh, that's what you call it."

"Alice."

"Stanley. Is that what you think? That I'm upset that you're interviewing the people I did? I'm not upset you're interviewing the same people I did. That's what you should do. That's how you're going to solve it."

"Solve it?"

"Of course you are. You're very good at this."

"Alice, we're not in New York. We're out in the bush. I don't know the people, and I haven't got a clue."

"Exactly. That's why you have to talk to people. So who'd you talk to at lunch?"

"The two librarians and the other married couple." I struggled to recall their names, figuring that would win me some points. "Simon and Trish," I said triumphantly.

Alice wasn't impressed. "Is that all? What about Keith and Jason? What about Annabel? Did you talk to them?"

"No, I didn't."

Alice nodded knowingly. "So. The only one I talked to that you talked to was Victoria. When you say I'm upset that you're talking to the same people I did, what you mean is I'm upset that you're talking to Victoria, the woman who was clinging to you like Saran Wrap."

"Actually, Saran Wrap doesn't cling as well as that stuff you get from Costco."

"Stanley, you have no idea when it's a good time to joke."

Actually, I do. With Alice it's never a good time to joke. I just can't help myself.

"I'll talk to them on the afternoon walk."

"They won't be on the afternoon walk. Clemson will mix it up again and we'll wind up walking with the librarians."

"No problem. I'll just say, no, no, I want to walk with the sexy nymphomaniac."

One look at Alice's face told me I'd found another bad time to joke.

24
DRIVE-HIKE

Clemson mixed it up in more ways than one. The afternoon walk was a drive-hike, which consisted of one of the jeeps dropping us off in the middle of nowhere and our having to find our way back to camp. I didn't know if that had already been on the schedule, or was just something Clemson made up on the spot.

He also mixed it up by coming along in our jeep. Alice and I had lucked out by being matched up with Victoria and Annabel and Keith and Jason again. It would have been the perfect situation for me to interview the suspects, with Alice helping out by distracting the other hikers when I wanted to get someone alone. Clemson scotched that by coming along. Duke was busy solving the Alice 2 murder, and Clemson was filling in for him. He carried a rifle and wore a ranger's uniform. I wondered if he was actually a ranger, or had just bought the outfit.

Our jeep was crowded. Lolita and her mother — excuse me, Victoria and Annabel — were in the front seat behind the driver. Keith and Jason had piled in behind them. Alice and I were in the back. John sat up front with one of the staff. I didn't know his name, but I knew he was one of the two who brought the hot water for the shower. He was along to drive the jeep back to camp. That left no room up front for Clemson, who sat with Victoria and Annabel. Daniel's replacement sat with Keith and Jason.

The drive was uneventful. We didn't see a lion, and no one got killed. Kind of a glass-half-full situation.

I have no idea how many kilometers we drove. I always convert them inaccurately to half-miles. Sorry, but I'm too old a dog to go metric.

After a good forty-five minutes, which included stopping too long for a few pedestrian sights — which was something in itself: the elephants and warthogs I had been so fascinated with a few days ago I now dismissed as commonplace — we pulled to a stop in a little clearing and all piled out.

The other jeep was nowhere in sight. No doubt it was because they were distracted by the sight of a lion standing over a fresh-killed zebra.

The water-bearing staff man hopped into the jeep and drove off with a bright smile and a cheery wave. I wondered if he had the faintest idea where he was going. I knew you could take your bearings from the sun, but the sun was never in the same spot. It was a good thing that responsibility was not mine.

John and the spotter conferred and then addressed us. At least John started to. Clemson jumped in and took charge, which as the ranger he had no right to do. But John wasn't about to protest.

"All right," Clemson said. "This should be fun."

I thought that was pushing it a little, what with a dead woman for breakfast. I wondered what Clemson thought would constitute merriment.

"This is farther from camp than we have ever been. It's virgin territory. If we find tracks, we will be the first to see them."

That was all well and good, but if we found tracks of a lion, all I cared about was whether they were two days old or fresh, not who saw them first.

I wondered if I'd be thinking such grouchy thoughts if there hadn't been a murder.

An alleged murder.

"Okay," Clemson said, "we're in a different location, but the same rules apply. John and I will go first, you follow in single file, you walk where we walk. And keep up. Phillip will be behind you. He doesn't have a cattle prod, but it's his job to make sure you don't lag behind. If he tells you to catch up, you do it."

"Do you know where camp is?" Annabel said.

Clemson smiled. "I ought to. It's my camp." He made a face, waved his hand self-deprecatingly. "I didn't mean that the way it sounded. I know where camp is, and so does John, and so does Phillip. We ought to be able to find it. If we don't, it will be your chance to find out what sausage fruit tastes like."

An impala trotted into the clearing, saw us, and froze. I could almost see the word "oops" forming on its rounded lips. It turned and bolted away.

"Gee, was it something I said?" I ventured.

Everyone looked amused but Clemson and Alice. Alice I'm used to, but Clemson was a bit of a surprise. Ordinarily, he'd be humoring the guests. I figured the situation was stressing him out. Of course I hadn't exactly been ingratiating myself with my suspicions of murder.

We set off through the underbrush, Clemson in the lead. He carried his rifle in his right hand, sticking out in front of him like a cutlass, as if he wouldn't have to shoot an attacking animal: he could dispatch it with a single thrust.

John was right over his shoulder, not willing to concede the leadership of the hike without at least a token resistance. Victoria and Annabel came next, followed by Keith and Jason, and Alice and me. Phillip brought up the rear.

We came into a clearing. Clemson held up his hand. We stopped. Looked around. Saw nothing. Heard nothing. What was Clemson doing? No one wanted to break the silence by asking. Clemson still had his hand up, his finger to his lips.

A cow on steroids came crashing through the bush. Not a cow-cow, but a steer, a bull, some big black horned animal the size of an SUV. The type that could trample you to death before you could figure out what it was.

I took a step back, looked to Alice. She was not only safe, she was calmly getting out her camera. The charging bull had

192

missed us and was stampeding through the clearing. I whipped off my backpack, grabbed the video camera, flipped the screen out, switched it on. Hoped it warmed up before the animal was out of sight. A shot of the retreating bull would go a long way toward demonstrating I was not brain-dead, which, as I get older, is more and more important. A picture appeared on the screen. I hit the Record button, caught the rear end of the animal as it galloped triumphantly into the underbrush.

In the viewfinder I could see Clemson, rifle in hand, looking not after the departing bull but into the thicket from whence it had come. The word *herd* leaped to mind. Herd of cattle. That's what stampedes, not one cow, a whole bunch.

I swung around to Alice, who suddenly seemed exposed. She wasn't, she was as out of the way as I was, but these things are relative.

"Stay back!" I said.

She gave me a look that might have felled the charging bull.

Belatedly, Clemson found his voice. "Careful! There may be more."

I checked out my fellow travelers. Victoria was on the ground. Keith had knocked her down, either in a movie star's heroic leap to save her, or in an opportunistic attempt to plaster his body against hers.

Victoria was squirming out from under him and did not look particularly pleased.

Annabel, who had not been knocked down, was shrieking as if her sister were being raped.

Jason looked the way he always looked, aloof and detached, though in his aviator shades it was hard to tell.

John looked completely relaxed. So did Clemson, aside from having the gun at the ready in case any more horned devils emerged from the bush.

None did. It was a frustrating hike. By the time we stopped for sundowners, we hadn't seen anything else of note, and I hadn't had a chance to question anyone.

I'd have liked to talk to Keith, but he was drooling over Victoria, and Annabel was having her usual tizzy and trying to break them up.

That left Jason, who was standing off to one side drinking a Coke Lite. He looked like he wanted to be left alone. I snuck up behind him, said, "Pretty exciting, eh?"

He turned, saw me, said, "What?"

"The bull, I mean. I don't mean the murder. That would be pretty ghoulish, calling the murder exciting."

Jason seemed annoyed that I was talking to him. "What murder? The woman died in her sleep."

"It still counts," I said. "They don't have to be wide awake when you kill them. You give a woman poison and she dies in her sleep, it's still a murder."

"No one gave her poison."

"How do you know? You know you didn't give her poison, but you can't speak for anybody else. Except maybe Keith. If you plan to provide him an alibi."

"I don't know what you're talking about."

Jason took a sip of Coke, made a face, dumped the rest out on the ground, and went over and set it on the table. I wasn't sure if he really hated the Coke, or if he'd just done it to get away from me. Granted, Coke Lite, the African version of Diet Coke, didn't taste exactly the same, but he'd been drinking it before I came over.

On the other hand, maybe he just wanted his hands free. He'd rolled up his sleeves to wash them in the bowl of water Phillip provided, and neglected to roll them down. Jason was obsessive about long sleeves and pants, probably because of bug bites.

His water bottle was slung over his shoulder and hung down his side. Naturally, now that I knew his name and didn't need to see

195

it, it faced out and said Jason.

I wondered if I should make another pass at him. I hadn't really asked a damn thing, and I was getting a guilty reaction.

I didn't. Bringing the murder up once could be casual. Twice would show a purpose.

Phillip was making Alice tea. I joined her in a cup, nibbled on a cookie that turned out to be largely sugar. Alice looked askance, as if I were committing sacrilege against the gods of nutrition.

I considered bothering the other hikers, but I just didn't have the heart for it. I marked my territory instead. I figured that was about as useful as the rest of my investigation.

It was getting dark, so we headed back, hoping to see something on the way.

We didn't. The bull was the only highlight of the whole hike. I figured Alice would be pleased with me for getting a shot of it.

She probably would have been if I'd remembered to turn off the camera instead of shooting forty-five minutes of my leg.

25
AUTOPSY REPORT

"You're an idiot."

"Thank you."

"Couldn't you remember to turn the camera off?"

"Don't I get any credit for turning it on?"

"I don't know. Did you shoot anything besides your leg?"

"Hang on. I gotta rewind."

When we got back to camp I had been surprised to find the video tape at the end. Rewinding a few minutes had told the story. My leg looked good, but probably wasn't worth forty-five minutes. In an act of cowardice, I had put the camera away until after dinner without telling Alice. We got back late and I was hungry. Once fed, I had confessed all.

I put the camera on rewind, waited impatiently for it to run through the entire tape.

"You're going to run down the battery."

"I beg your pardon?"

"You filmed for an hour, now you're rewinding without the camera plugged in. You'll be lucky if you have any battery left."

I looked at the gauge. The battery was low. I cursed Alice's rightness. How dare she be so damn right. The battery was going to run out and it would be my fault.

I stopped the tape, even though it had not completely rewound. The charging bull was not the first thing I'd filmed. The problem was I didn't know how many minutes I'd taken. If I'd shot around a half an hour, the charging bull would be right here. It wasn't. I had a nice action shot of my right leg walking along the trail.

I stopped, hit rewind again. Wound it back about five minutes, stopped and hit play. Another leg shot. This one had a better view of my boot, probably not significant.

"If you keep looking at footage, you're going to run down the battery," Alice said.

"You want me to go charge it?"

"Of course not. You'd get eaten by a lion."

I sighed, hit rewind.

"Did you take your Malarone?" Alice said.

I had not taken my Malarone. I set the camera on the bed, dug deep in my backpack, pulled out my daily pill minder, a rectangular plastic pill case with seven compartments labeled Sunday through

Saturday. Without it, I might suspect I had taken my Malarone, but I wouldn't really know.

I still wasn't completely sure, because in the bush it wasn't easy to know what day it was. Asking Alice would only invite scorn. By the time I did a calculation only slightly less complicated than $E = mc^2$ and figured out I hadn't taken my Malarone and duly took it, the tape had rewound all the way.

Now I was totally screwed in the opposite direction. The way to find the bull was to fast forward a few minutes, then hit play to see how close I thought I was to it. I knew what Alice would think about that. Another was to put the camera on play, hold the fast forward down, and skim through the footage while at least seeing where I was on the tape. I wondered how much battery that would take. More to the point, I wondered how much battery Alice would *think* that would take.

The easy way was just to turn the tape on and watch it. I wondered if I should do that.

The camera solved the problem for me by shutting off. The screen went dark. I looked for the icon to see how much battery was left. The icon was gone. The camera was stone dead.

I switched it off, looked over at Alice. She

had that triumphant I-told-you-so/married-a-moron look. Any wife can do one. It takes sheer artistry to do both at once. I hate to brag, but Alice is second to none.

"Is the battery dead?" Alice said.

"I was almost there."

"Well, if you hadn't turned the camera on and off so many times."

"Sorry. I'll show you the bull tomorrow."

"Water buffalo," Alice corrected. She got no points for it. Clemson had ID'd the beast for us once the peril was past. "Assuming you pointed the camera at it. Considering how obsessed you are with your right leg."

"Did you get any shots of it?"

"They're no good."

"Let's see."

Alice had already transferred them to the iPad. I could see what she meant. The shots were in focus, but all they showed was the buffalo's hindquarters vanishing into the bush. I was sure mine wouldn't be any better.

"Well, now you know to charge your camera," Alice said.

I said nothing, sat and took it.

"Knock, knock."

It was a voice outside our tent. I looked at Alice, said, "Come in."

Clemson ducked under the flap. He didn't

look happy. No surprise there. He hadn't looked happy in some time.

"Something up?" I said.

"Yeah. I'll have to tell the others tomorrow. I wanted to talk to you first."

"Tell them what?"

"Alice Ardsdale was poisoned."

"That's not surprising."

"Maybe not, but it's certainly bad news. A lot will depend on how it's handled. I was hoping you could help."

"By keeping my mouth shut?"

Alice shot me a warning glance. I took the point. Antagonizing Clemson was probably not in our best interests. "What do you want me to do?"

He grimaced. "It's an unfortunate situation. I can't have people panic, but I can't withhold this from them. It all will depend on how it's presented. You can help me with that. Because you have experience in this area. You've dealt with homicides before."

"You're conceding it's a homicide."

"It's hard to deny in the face of the medical findings."

"That she was poisoned?"

"Yes."

"And not accidentally?"

"I'm afraid not. I had hope for the poison plant. Unfortunately, someone slipped her a whacking dose of arsenic."

"What?"

"I'm afraid that's right." Clemson exhaled. "You mind if I sit down? I'm exhausted." Without waiting for permission, he sat on the end of my cot. "So the accidental theory doesn't fly. It was murder. You see why I need to count on your discretion?"

"Wait a minute," Alice said. "You come in here, you tell us a woman's been murdered, and you ask us to be discreet? Are you out of your mind? This is not something you hush up. People who hush up murders go to jail."

Clemson put up his hands. "No one's asking you to hush up anything. People must be told. Nothing must be withheld. That's what I said to begin with. It just matters how they're told."

"We're not spin doctors either," I said.

"Of course you're not. We're getting far afield. You ought to hear me out before you raise your objections."

That remark seemed dangerously close to criticizing Alice for jumping in. She bristled, but held her tongue.

"Fine, give us the spiel," I said. "We're promising nothing, we're just listening. Okay?"

"Okay. Alice died in her sleep. She was

202

poisoned the night before. She went to bed, never woke up. At first glance it would appear that she was poisoned at dinner, and nothing in the medical report contradicts that. But there are many other possibilities for the poison."

"For instance?"

"Her water bottle, for one. We all have individual water bottles. They all have our names on them. Easy enough to poison her water bottle, knowing she'd get it."

"Or *I* would," Alice said. "The bottles are not distinctive enough. I've taken her bottle off the table more than once."

"Well, thank goodness you didn't. We don't know if the poison was in the bottle, but it's certainly likely."

"Likely?" I said. "How can you say likely? Was there poison in the bottle or not?"

"That remains to be seen."

"What are you talking about? Can't you tell?"

"Not without drinking some," Clemson said. "We have no testing facilities in camp. The bottle's on its way to the lab in Lusaka. We should have results by tomorrow."

"Oh, for goodness sakes."

"But that's just one possibility. There are others. Someone could have given her the poison. In a drink, in food, or even as a medical dose."

"Medical dose?"

"We're in the wild. Bathroom facilities are limited. People underestimate what a change in diet, climate, even time zone will do to their digestive system. Pepto-Bismol should mask just about anything. People tend to chug Pepto-Bismol right down, rather than sip it."

"Did she have Pepto-Bismol?"

"No. That doesn't mean she didn't borrow some. That's what I mean by being unprepared."

"That's ridiculous."

"Why?"

"She's investigating a murder, and she asks one of the suspects for a dose of medicine?"

Clemson beamed. "See? That's why I need *you* to interpret the evidence. You have the experience to point out how certain things are illogical. The whole borrow-the-dose-of-medicine theory, for instance."

"It was your theory."

"It's not my theory. It's one possible explanation. It happens to be a bad one, as you so ably pointed out."

"I don't suppose you'd care to suggest a better theory?"

Alice put up her hands. "Boys. Boys. Let's

not make this a pissing contest. You were trying to tell us about the evidence. Not some wild interpretation of it that you don't even believe. Am I correct in my assessment that the woman was poisoned with arsenic, and there's no concrete evidence indicating how the poison was delivered?"

"Your wife has a good grasp of the situation," Clemson said.

"That makes one of us. I still don't know what you want."

"I want an investigator on the inside. I want someone who can talk to the others without arousing suspicion. It won't be hard. Once it gets out that she was poisoned, it will be the topic of discussion."

"No kidding."

"I want to take advantage of that. I want you to conduct interrogations without anyone knowing it."

"Everyone knows I'm a PI. I've already been asking questions."

"Yes, but they won't know you're doing it for me."

"Wait a minute. Won't the police be conducting their own investigations?"

"What police?"

"Didn't you say with the murder of an American citizen the consulate would step in?"

"They will. But they're not here. And they're unlikely to send anyone until an analysis of the evidence is complete. In the meantime, Duke is in charge."

It was all I could do not to scoff. Duke might have the authority, but I knew damn well who was in charge.

"Duke will be questioning us?"

"Absolutely. There is another area where you could help. You've been involved in police investigations before. The others haven't. You could reassure them that just because a policeman is asking them questions doesn't mean they're under suspicion."

"So tomorrow's hike is canceled?"

"Not exactly."

26
INTERROGATIONS

It was the talk of breakfast.

"I don't understand," the other husband said. I still had to remind myself his name was Simon.

The news had spread like wildfire. Not that Alice and I had leaked it. Someone else had found out from some other source. It was impossible to know who, but by the time I got to breakfast after a visit to the straight-drop toilet for a hearty rendition of The Twelve Days of Malarone, everybody knew. Not an auspicious start to my career as a clandestine investigator.

"There's nothing to understand," Trish said. She looked exasperated. She also looked good this morning in a crisply ironed safari shirt. She must have had it in her bag. No one was doing any ironing. "She was poisoned. We thought she was, now we know she was. Same difference."

"It can't have anything to do with us,"

Hells Angel #2 said. I temporarily relegated her to the status of Non-Edith Librarian.

"Why?" I said.

"Why? Because it's got nothing to do with us. Do you think I killed her? Do you think Edith did?"

"Of course not. But an outsider, who doesn't know us, might think anything."

"Like what?" Annabel said. "You mean like someone's after us?"

Victoria rolled her eyes.

"No one's after us," Keith said. I could practically see him seizing the opportunity to ingratiate himself with Victoria. "We're not the ones making trouble."

"You think Alice was making trouble?" Non-Edith Librarian said.

"Do you think she was killed for poking into Daniel's death?" Victoria said.

Non-Edith Librarian shrugged. "That makes more sense than anything else."

That prompted a rash of conversation, several people talking at once. So far, the only one not to venture an opinion was Keith's roommate, Jason, who looked sullen. It seemed to be his default position.

Clemson came walking up with a piece of toast, a useful prop that grounded him in reality, made it seem like this was just another day. "I gather you've all heard," he said. "The rumors are true. Alice was poisoned, we have to investigate it, and yes, our schedule is changed. But let me assure you that no one thinks any of you had anything to do with it. Duke will be asking questions this morning. Try not to take offense. It doesn't mean he suspects you. It means he wants to get whatever information you might have that could shed some light on this dreadful situation. It affects our schedule. The morning hike is canceled." That announcement produced, if not a protest, at least a murmur of dissatisfaction. "I know, I know. These things happen. We'll have a game drive instead. It'll be shorter than normal, but we have to get back here in time."

"In time for what?" Keith said.

"In time to pack up and move out of our tents."

That announcement was greeted with shock and hostility.

"You mean the rest of the trip is canceled?" Keith said.

"Not at all. We're just changing the schedule. I checked with the next camp. They're set up to receive us. We're moving the canoe trip up a day."

The murmurs this time were of approval. The canoe trip was the highlight of the tour.

"So," Clemson said, "after the morning drive you come back, you pack, you go to lunch. Be completely packed, because during lunch everything will be moved to the jeeps. After lunch we head out."

"Where?" Annabel said.

"Zimbabwe," Clemson said. "It's in your itinerary. Just move everything up a day. We drive to Victoria Falls, cross over the border. Tomorrow morning we have canoe lessons and set out on the river."

"Just like that?" Annabel said. "But we're not ready."

"We'll practice with the canoes. If you can paddle, fine. If you really can't do it, you can go with me."

"They're two-man canoes?" Simon, the other husband, said.

"That's right," Clemson said. "It wouldn't be safe for singles. We have too large a group. We'd be too spread out to supervise. But we'll go over all that when we get there. Finish your breakfast, then hang around here so Duke can talk to you."

"I need to go back to the tent," Trish, the other wife, said. I figured that was a euphemism for straight-drop toilet.

Clemson heard it that way too. "No problem. Go back to the tent, visit the bathroom, take anything you need for the drive, and come back here and talk to Duke. Just don't wander away."

That set off a stampede. Half the people bolted for their tents, whether to use the facilities or just to get away from Duke. I found myself sitting next to Alice.

"Going back to the tent?" I said.

"I don't have a guilty conscience."

"It doesn't mean they do." I looked around at who was left. "By those standards, the other husband and you and I and the two librarians are all innocent."

"Speak for yourself," Alice said. She got up and headed for the tent.

Simon got up and left too. Leaving me with the two librarians. That wasn't good. The librarians were mystery readers. Alice 2 had been a mystery reader, and Alice 2 wound up dead. That didn't mean the librarians were next to go, but the fact that they hadn't exhibited a guilty conscience cast them in the role of victims.

"Stanley?"

I looked up.

A staff man, one of the two who brought shower water, was standing in front of me. I was surprised he knew my name.

"Yes?" I said.

"Come."

It took a moment to process the information that he wanted me to go with him. I got up, followed him through the underbrush to the staff campsite.

Duke sat in a folding chair in front of one of the tents. There was another chair facing it. He pointed to it, said "Sit."

I sat, waited for my interrogation to begin. I wondered what it would be like. So far I hadn't heard Duke say much more than sausage fruit.

Duke watched my escort walk away. He turned back to me, flashed entirely too many white teeth for an interrogation, and said, "Why do you think it's one of you?"

27
DUKE

I couldn't believe he'd said that. I'd expected some monosyllabic interrogation of no consequence whatsoever. Instead, he'd jumped right to the heart of the matter.

"What?"

"The guests. The tourists. You think they killed Daniel."

"I never said that."

"Alice said that. Now she is dead."

I struggled to adjust to the embarrassment of my prejudices kicking me in the ass, assuming Duke wasn't particularly sharp.

"You think that's why she was killed?"

"I'm interested in what you think."

"It seems logical," I said.

"Logical?"

"That means it could happen."

"Yes, it could happen. Do you think it happened?"

"Yes, I do."

"Why?"

"Two people are killed on the same tour. I don't think one is a murder and one is an accident."

He nodded. "Yes. You think there is a killer. You think the killer is one of the guests."

"She was questioning the guests."

"Yes. She was questioning the staff too."

I stared at him. "What?"

"Clemson tells me I can talk to you."

"Oh."

"Clemson says you have experience. That does not mean you are not the killer."

"Yeah. Well, I happen to know I'm not, which gives me an advantage."

"What?"

"I didn't do it. Go on. What about her questioning the staff?"

"I can tell you things if you do not tell the guests. If you tell the guests, it would be very bad."

"You already told me about her questioning the staff."

"Yes. And you should not tell the guests."

Duke had something to learn about getting a promise of confidentiality *before* divulging information, but I wasn't about to make an issue of it.

"Fine," I said. "What else am I not supposed to tell the guests?"

"Daniel sold drugs."

My mouth fell open. "Is that true?"

"Yes. Some boys do. They are poor. Pay is not high."

"Clemson knew this?"

"He did not know then. He knows now."

"How did you find out?"

"I asked."

"And they told you?"

"They did not want to."

I waited for an explanation, but none was forthcoming. I was becoming increasingly impressed with Duke's interrogation methods.

"You think he was killed over drugs?"

"It happens. Does it happen in your country?"

"All the time. Who told you Daniel sold drugs?"

"David is bad liar."

"David?"

"The boy who brought you. His name is David."

"Does David use drugs?"

"He says no."

"Do you believe him?"

Duke shrugged. "Boys use drugs."

"Was Alice talking to David?"

"David, and Daniel, and Phillip, and Carl."

"Carl?"

"You have seen him. He works with David."

"Are you telling me she came over here and questioned the staff?"

"No. The boys bring water. They bring food. They build fires. She talks to them there."

"How do you know?"

"I asked."

"What did she ask them about?"

"Daniel. Who are his friends? Was he in trouble? Did he need money?"

"What did they tell her?"

"They did not tell her about drugs."

"How do you know?"

"That is what they say."

"They may lie."

"They do not need to lie. She does not ask, they do not say."

"They may lie to you."

"No. They tell me about drugs."

"They may lie to you when they say they didn't tell her. If they told her about the drugs and didn't want you to know, they could say they didn't."

"Why? She does not say drugs, they do not say drugs."

"Then why was she killed?"

He nodded. "That is problem."

"Then you do think it's one of us."

"No."

"She didn't ask about drugs. She asked about Daniel."

"They do not care about drugs. They care about murder."

I took a breath. I was having trouble leading Duke through if-then relationships. Now that I knew he was sharp, I didn't know if that was because he really didn't follow, or whether he was being intentionally obtuse.

Clemson stepped out of the tent and said, "I'll take it from here."

28
2ND INTERROGATION

"You were listening the whole time?"

"Yes."

"Do you intend to listen in on all the interrogations?"

"No, just yours."

"Am I supposed to feel flattered?"

"You can if you like. That wasn't the idea."

"What was the idea?"

"I want to talk to you about the murder."

"You did that last night."

"Yes, yes. Your wife was there. We were talking generally. I was adjusting to the news. I want to talk to you alone."

We were in sitting on the cots in Clemson's tent. He had two of them, standard issue, though he bunked alone. He was using the second one for his duffle, which was open with clothes and equipment strewn around. He had cleared a space for me to sit on the cot, sat facing me on his.

"What did you want to talk about?" I said.

"Let's not play games," Clemson said. "We have a serious situation here. A tourist has been murdered. That's bad enough. If another tourist did it, it's worse."

"Why?"

"It shuts me down. The police step in. And not just the local police. We're talking about the government. The consulate's involved. The next thing you know, you have an international incident."

"I would think it was the other way around. You'd have an international incident if a tourist was killed by a Zambian."

"Yes, but one that's easily resolved. We apologize. We don't know how this deplorable situation could have occurred, but we're dreadfully sorry and we will take steps to see that it never happens again. Some poor bloke is arrested and quickly put on trial if he's guilty, or lost somewhere in the legal system if he's not. And a crisis is averted and order is restored."

"Are you really as cynical as all that?"

He grinned, pointed his finger. "Got me. No, but you get the point. If a tourist killed a tourist, it's a circus and it shuts me down. That's clearly not what happened. Daniel was involved with drugs and wound up getting killed. Most likely by someone else on the staff who wanted his drugs, wanted his business, got high and couldn't control himself. Alice Ardsdale was poking into it. Asking questions of the staff. The killer doesn't realize she's asking questions of everybody, he thinks she's after him. So he feeds her poison. Not that hard to do, if he's one of the boys who serves the food."

"Where's he get arsenic?"

"It's used in copper mining."

"Mining?"

"You know nothing about this country, do you? Copper mining is a major industry. That's why China wants the land. But you know nothing about that either. Never mind. The point is, the idea that a staff man did this is not farfetched. It is most likely true."

"It's stuffy in here. Can't we sit outside?"

"I don't want the others to see you."

"Why not?"

"I want them to talk to you freely. I don't want them to think you're reporting back to me. You're my eyes and ears on the ground."

"Why?"

"What?"

"If you really think one of the staff did it, why do you want me to talk to the guests?"

"I have to protect against that outcome. It may not be likely, but it's possible. If that should turn out to be the case, I need it cleaned up as quickly and efficiently as possible. It shouldn't be that difficult."

"I beg your pardon."

"There's either a killer or there's not. Among the guests, I mean. The only way of finding that out is to find out who it is. See what I mean?"

I did. There was a kernel of truth behind Clemson's twisted logic.

"So that's your job," Clemson said.

I frowned. "Isn't that Duke's job?"

"Yes, it is. But he won't be along."

"What?"

"The ranger doesn't go on the canoe trip. Neither do the guides. I function as both guide and ranger. The only other staff man in the canoes is a spotter we pick up there."

I frowned.

"So I want you to talk to the guests."

"People will know I'm investigating."

"Of course they will. That's fine. They just won't know you're doing it for me."

"Assuming that we go."

"What?"

"You're assuming the canoe trip goes out. When the lab finishes analyzing the evidence, aren't they apt to hold you here and send someone?"

"No one could get here that fast."

"They could call and tell you to wait."

His eyes flicked.

I've been involved in enough investigations to know a guilty reaction when I saw one. "You turned your phone off, didn't you? No one's getting through until you're safely out on the river."

Clemson started to protest, realized it was futile. "All right, look," he said. "Here's the thing. I can't afford to shut down, even for a day. My profit margin is razor-thin. Next to nothing. If everything goes smoothly, I'm fine. Any glitch and I'm screwed. The trip's a washout. Might even cost me money."

"Why don't you charge more?"

He made a face. "I'm not Wilderness Adventure. I'm not Thompson Safari. If I raise my fee, people book with them. I don't have gourmet meals and luxury lodges. I have low overhead and I'm cheap."

I knew that. Alice had investigated all tours before going. This was the one we could afford.

"So," Clemson said, "you talk to the guests, and Duke will talk to the staff. He pulled their records. David had a drug bust as a juvenile. Marijuana, no big deal, but it's there. Carl got in a fight in town. He lost *and* paid a fine. Phillip's record is clean, but he has a wife, three children, could need money."

"Phillip has a wife?"

"Yes."

"He looks twelve."

"He's about twenty. No evidence of violence or crime, but he could need money."

"What about the guides?"

"No one thinks it's the guides, but in light of the evidence, Duke's pulling their records. It's what he'll be doing while we're gone. He'll also be making inquiries in town. If there's anything there, he'll dig it up."

I cocked my head. "Duke's rather sharp. I thought you told me he'd only solved one murder case."

Clemson shrugged. "We don't have many."

29
SHORT GAME DRIVE

The game drive was a joke. I don't know the punch line, but the setup was how do you keep ten tourists pissed off for hours? The answer was cancel the morning hike and have them interrogated by a Zambian ranger feigning a lack of English.

I knew that because I went first, so I was free to hang out at the campfire and greet the other guests as they returned. None came back happy. Unfortunately, none came back communicative. At least about the murder. Several were relatively vocal concerning Duke's investigative techniques, verbal skills, intelligence, and parentage, then retired to their tents to sulk until the game drive.

Victoria was one of the last. As she walked by afterwards, I said, "Don't worry. I didn't give you up."

She frowned. "What?"

"That was a joke."

"Oh. Very funny."

"So what did he ask?"

"Same thing he asked you."

I doubted that. "You mean like the last time you saw her alive?"

"He didn't put it that succinctly."

"I'm shocked. What did you tell him?"

"I don't remember."

"You don't remember what you told him?"

"No, I don't remember the last time I saw her alive. Probably at dinner like everyone else."

"Is that what everyone else said?"

"I have no idea what anyone else said."

"Except me."

"Huh?"

"You said he asked you the same thing he asked me."

"He probably did. I have no idea." She frowned. "Are you checking my statement?"

"Why would I do that?"

"I have no idea. Are you?"

"Any reason you'd tell me anything different than you told him?"

"Did he tell you to check on the guests?"

"No, just you."

She crinkled up her nose. God help me, she looked adorable. "Did he really?"

"No, that was a joke."

"Good one," she said. "Did you question Jason?"

"He didn't stop by."

"I'm not surprised."

"Why?"

"He didn't look too happy when he came out," she said, and walked off to her tent.

It took a while for her remark to register. When he came out? So Duke must have moved the questioning inside the tent after Clemson and I were gone. And David must have been picking up the guests one by one. He'd leave a guest outside the tent to be interrogated after the one inside was through, and go back to get another. So some of the guests were alone outside the tent while others were being questioned, and might have listened in. Victoria could have listened in on Jason. And Jason could have listened in on the guest ahead of him. Who was that? Could I remember the sequence?

By the time I got back from my talk with Clemson, the questioning was under way. The first people back were Simon and Trish. Trish came first, then Simon. So he could have listened in on her. Then came the librarians. I wasn't sure which was first. So one could have listened in on the other, and one could have listened in on Simon.

Next up was Keith, who could have listened in on one of the librarians. Then came Jason, who could have listened in on Keith. What if he had? Something Keith said could have been what pissed him off. Maybe that was what made him grumpy, rather than his own interrogation. Of course, it wasn't an either/or situation. The guy was just generally grumpy.

But Victoria had remarked on it. So it must have been blatant. Of course she could have listened in on *him* and known exactly what was bothering him. But I didn't think so. She hadn't shown a single guilty reaction. And she'd volunteered the information. If she'd learned it from spying, she wouldn't have brought it up.

While I was thinking all that, Annabel came back.

"Well, that wasn't so bad, was it?" I said. With Annabel I figured a cheery approach was best. Not that I expected it to work.

It didn't.

"Pointless," she sniffed. "I don't know anything."

"Who's next?"

"Huh?"

"Who's in there now?"

"I think I'm last," she said, and headed for her tent.

She was last? Funny. Seemed like there was somebody else.

Oh, yes.

Alice.

I went back to our tent.

Alice was there.

"Did you talk to Duke?"

"Yeah. Surprised I didn't see you."

"I was talking to Clemson."

"Why?"

"Duke didn't tell you?"

"Tell me what?"

I gave Alice a rundown of my talk with Clemson.

"He wants you to be his spy?"

"Duke didn't tell you?"

"Duke didn't tell me anything. He could barely formulate the questions."

"That's an act. He's actually articulate."

"You're kidding."

"You couldn't tell?"

"Not in a million years."

My estimation of Duke's prowess soared. It wasn't easy to put one over on Alice.

"He didn't ask you anything?"

"Just a few basic questions. Like the last time I saw her alive."

"He didn't ask any follow-ups?"

"Not of any depth. He acted like he wouldn't have understood the answers."

"He just asked when?"

"He wrote down the time. Very laboriously. Then read it back to be sure he got it right."

"He should get an Oscar nod. I guess that's his plan. Just lock down a few facts, see if I can come up with anything that contradicts them."

"Not much of a plan."

"It's largely for show. Clemson doesn't think it's one of us. I gotta pack."

"You're packed."

I looked. My duffle and backpack were lined up ready to go. Alice had packed for me while she was waiting. She seemed surprised I ever thought she wouldn't.

A voice outside the tent announced game drive.

Alice handed me my binoculars harness, which she'd laid out on the bed. "Come on. Let's spot a lion."

We didn't. The game drive was perfunctory at best. Interrogations hadn't taken that long and we got a decent start; still it was short. It also seemed rushed. Like the guides weren't trying all that hard to spot any animals.

We got back, had a hasty lunch, and piled into the jeeps again.

As we drove away, I could have sworn I

saw Duke run out into the parking lot, waving his arms.

30
VICTORIA FALLS

We crossed the border at Victoria Falls. We
were not alone. Everyone crosses the border
at Victoria Falls. Zambia and Zimbabwe
border on the Zambezi River, and the only
way to cross the river is the bridge at Victoria Falls. Well, the only legitimate way.
You can also swim the crocodile-infested
river, but they don't recommend it. The
guides, I mean. The crocodiles don't mind.

It's an awesome bridge. Victoria Falls is
one of the largest waterfalls in the world.
Locals will tell you it *is* the largest, considering height, width, and water mass. I don't
know about that, but it's one big falls.

We had our visas stamped at border
patrol, lugged our bags over the bridge. Our
vehicles weren't coming. The drivers had no
visas. A tour bus was meeting us on the
other side.

Keith flexed his muscles and tried to help
Victoria with her duffle, but she was having

none of it. I'd have been glad to let him take mine, but he didn't offer.

Clemson, who'd been uncharacteristically quiet during the drive, seemed to loosen up once we were on the bridge.

"Anyone like bungee jumps?" he asked. "Take a look down. This is one of the best bungee jumps in the world."

"Do we have the time to do it?" Keith said.

I hoped we did. He'd have to, just so as to not back down in front of Victoria.

"It's expensive," Clemson said.

"How expensive?"

"A hundred and thirty-five dollars."

"For one jump?" I said.

Victoria smiled. "Oh? You're going to jump twice?"

"Not at those prices," I said.

Keith gave me such a look. Without even trying, I'd stolen his thunder.

Clemson's eyes twinkled. "It's free if you jump nude."

"Really?"

"Yeah, you jump naked and they don't charge you."

"Oh, great, I can afford it," Victoria said.

"All right!" Keith said loutishly.

I restrained my own loutish reaction. I knew Victoria had only said it for Annabel's benefit. "How high is it?" I said.

232

"The bridge is one hundred and eight meters."

I started doing the math.

"That's three hundred and fifty-four feet," Clemson said. He pointed to me. "You were figuring it out, weren't you?"

"You caught me. I was converting it to football fields. It's one point oh eight."

Alice rolled her eyes and shook her head, but Victoria laughed appreciatively.

"That would be a hundred and eight *yards*," Keith said scornfully. "It's a hundred and eight *meters*."

I threw up my hands. "Then I *clearly* can't jump."

Even Alice laughed at that.

Keith was frustrated, and it didn't get any better for him when one of the librarians said, "Come on, Edith. Whaddya say? Wanna jump?"

Edith laughed. "I don't know. Can we jump together?"

"They wouldn't let you," Clemson said. "Particularly since that girl fell."

"Since what?" Annabel exclaimed.

"The bungee cord snapped and a girl fell in the river. Wasn't killed, just banged up a bit. The miracle was that the crocodiles didn't eat her."

No one bungee-jumped.

We lugged our duffles to the Zimbabwe side of the bridge and cleared customs. Clemson talked to them for us. I'm not sure if money changed hands, but no one looked in our bags. Not that it would have mattered, unless someone wanted to bust me for trafficking in Malarone.

Our tour bus turned out to be a converted school bus with all the amenities of an ox cart. Our driver was a little old man who seemed determined to make up for the fact that our other drivers hadn't shown enough white teeth. Either that or he had just won the lottery, in which case I couldn't imagine why he was driving this bus.

It was small. We all fit, but just barely. I couldn't help wondering how we'd have made it if Alice 2 hadn't been bumped off. No, I did not voice the thought.

We left Victoria Falls, a booming tourist trap, and soon were bumping along occasionally paved roads though less developed areas.

It was our first real experience on an African roadway. From Lusaka we'd flown straight into the middle of nowhere. But now we were driving through inhabited terrain. This ranged from small towns with more traditional, if modest, structures made from recognizable building materials including one-room stores displaying signs boasting of Coca-Cola, filling stations dispensing liters of petrol, and a few private homes, to the outskirts where families lived in one-room shacks and women and children lined the road selling fruit and firewood.

Against all odds, there were occasional traffic jams, probably owing to the narrowness of the roadway and Zimbabwean drivers' insistence on passing whether there was anything coming or not. Often I would be treated to the horrifying spectacle of four cars racing head-on at each other. Miraculously, none collided.

"Are there ever accidents?" I asked Clemson when I had calmed down enough to take my heart out of my mouth.

"Oh, all the time," he said. "It's a real nuisance, because then the roads are blocked."

"Glad I asked."

We didn't crash, and soon we were driving down a dirt road through open terrain. I relaxed and scanned the horizon, hoping for a lion.

"Are there more lions in Zimbabwe than Zambia?" I asked Clemson.

He laughed. "Don't worry. We'll see a lion."

"We'd better," Trish said. "We didn't

come all this way not to see a lion."

"I'm sure you came for other things besides that," Clemson said.

"That's all well and good," Trish said. "But I want to see a lion."

We all agreed with that. I continued looking for one, but none appeared.

It was getting dark. I was looking forward to camp. After several days in the bush, I was eager to get back to the luxuries of the first day's camp with real bathrooms and showers and an actual dinner table.

It certainly would have been nice. Our camp, when the two jeeps that met our bus pulled into it, was a bush camp just like the one we'd left behind, with a campfire, and primitive tents, and, so help me, a straight-drop toilet.

Dinner was chicken and rice. They'd also made a salad, but they needn't have bothered. No one touched it.

There was also a hot-water-bag shower, but I doubt if anyone used it. Alice and I certainly didn't. It had been a long day, and we had to be out early on the river.

Just as I was falling asleep, it occurred to me that since we had left Zambia, no one, including Clemson, had alluded to the death of Alice 2.

31
CANOE LESSON

"All right," Clemson said. "Let's try it. Remember, the stern man does most of the paddling. The bow man hardly has to paddle at all. Most of the time you don't. The bow man watches where the canoe is going, tells the stern man when to turn."

I wish he hadn't said that. We were on the river having our first and only canoe lesson. I was in the stern and Alice was in the bow. Suggesting Alice tell me what to do was kind of like enabling an alcoholic.

We were all in two-man canoes. Clemson was alone in his, sitting in the stern. He dipped his paddle in the water, and the canoe shot ahead. He dipped it again, swung around to face us.

"Now, you can't just paddle on one side or the canoe will go around in circles. But you don't change after every stroke or you'd wear yourself out. A few paddles on one side, and when the canoe starts to turn you switch over."

"Paddle left," Alice said.

I couldn't believe it. I hadn't even dipped the paddle. This was not going to go well.

It didn't. No matter how many strokes I did, it was always one too many or one too few. I wouldn't have known this, but Alice was quick to point it out.

I was not alone. Every canoe had a back-seat driver in the front seat, and most were not shy about venturing opinions. Annabel was certain Victoria was trying to tip her out. And Trish wasn't handing Simon any trophies either. Jason, as usual, couldn't have cared less, but Keith whizzed along dexterously, trying to impress Victoria. Only the librarians appeared to be learning.

"Well," Clemson said. "That was terrible. None of you are ready to go out on the river. I'd be insane to take you. Luckily I am insane, so you get another chance. All of you are having trouble keeping the canoe going straight. Here's a little trick. At the end of your stroke, instead of taking your paddle out of the water, turn it sideways, like this. The water drags against the paddle, acts as a rudder, straightens the canoe out. You don't hold it there long because it slows the canoe and you'll turn too far. And you don't do it on every stroke. A few strokes, the canoe starts to go, you turn the paddle sideways, and you're right back stroking. I'm not saying you never switch to the other side, of course you do, and when you want to go fast you should be pulling as many strokes as possible and not creating a drag. But paddling along, nice and lazy, turn the paddle, give yourself a rest. Okay, let's give it a try."

A full recap of Alice's assessment of my attempt can be found in Wikipedia under Unmitigated Disasters. She also insisted on demonstrating the proper technique from the bow. The stroke wasn't designed for the bow. This tended to make our canoe go nowhere. Within minutes, everyone else was on one side of the river and we were on the other.

"Do stay with the group," Clemson called.

I gritted my teeth, paddled in that direction.

"Now then," Clemson said. "Right here the river is wide, the current is gentle. But when the current's strong and the wind is blowing hard, the canoe is going to run into the bank. When the bow hits the bank it stops and the stern keeps going. Do you know what you do then?"

"Paddle on the other side to straighten out," I ventured.

I shouldn't have.

"No," Clemson said. "You don't do that at all. It won't work and you'll just get yourself stuck. Let the stern of the canoe swing around. Paddle to help it along. Let the canoe do a full three sixty until you're facing forward again. Now, let's see you bump into the bank and turn around."

Even with Alice's instructions I had no problem running into the bank. The rest of the turn was a bit of an adventure. Alice didn't want me to help it along. She didn't want me to interfere with the good work the current was doing. The result was chaos.

In this instance we were not alone. The other husband and wife got tangled in a low-hanging bush, Annabel and Victoria's canoe wound up going backwards, Keith got so exuberant showing off that he overshot and went around twice. Only the two librarians did it right. They appeared to be having no problem whatsoever.

After about twenty minutes Clemson suggested that anyone who wanted should switch seats and let the other one paddle. Only the librarians took him up on the option. The change made no difference. They remained the only team to consistently paddle well.

"All right," Clemson said, when the lesson was over. "None of you are wonderful. None of you are even competent. Except Edith and Pam."

Another name learned, I thought triumphantly. Non-Edith Librarian was Pam. That had to be everyone.

"You can all do it to some extent. At least enough not to warrant leaving you behind. If there's anyone who thinks they really can't do it, they can go with me."

"I'll go with you," Alice said.

Clemson looked at her in surprise. "But you're in the bow. You don't have to paddle."

"No, but he does. Trust me, riding with him is not going to be good for my mental health."

Alice can say incredibly insulting things about me with absolute impunity. By smiling and presenting it in a humorous manner, she has reduced degrading one's husband to a work of art. She is seen as a tolerant, forgiving, long-suffering saint, coping with her husband's shortcomings. I am seen as a lovable buffoon.

"Let's see what we can do about that," Clemson said. "Is there anyone who feels they absolutely cannot paddle?"

No one confessed to that failing.

"All right," Clemson said. "Then there is no problem. You can ride with me."

I must admit I felt a momentary surge of relief at being freed from the clutches of a relentless taskmaster. It was short-lived, however. With Alice riding with Clemson, there was no one to ride with me. And I couldn't go alone, there weren't enough canoes. I had to double up.

The only other person who didn't have a partner was a young Zimbabwean who was going along as Clemson's assistant. His name was Bono, which I liked, because I could remember it. I can't say I liked Bono. He was the first sour African I had met in either country. He was particularly uncommunicative and never opened his mouth except to complain. I was not thrilled at the prospect of being partnered with him.

It was worse than I thought. Bono was the experienced canoe paddler, so naturally he sat in the stern. I had to sit in the bow.

I couldn't paddle at all.

32
ROLLIN' ON A RIVER

The early going was uneventful. I'm sure they plan it that way. Launch the canoes in a spot where nothing much is happening.

It was a positively idyllic scene. The blue water, the green vegetation on the banks. Six canoes gliding along single-file. The kind of shot you'd expect to see on the cover of a travel brochure.

I was filming it with my movie camera. I had nothing else to do. I was sitting in the bow of Bono's canoe, not paddling. I tried paddling for a while, but Bono stopped me. "Don't paddle," he said. "I paddle."

It was enough to give me a complex, first Alice telling me not to paddle and then Bono. In his case I understood. Paddling in the bow can wreak havoc with paddling in the stern, throw an expert like Bono off his course. Fine with me, I had nothing to prove. I dug out the video camera.

I'd charged the battery during the morning game drive, after Duke finished questioning the guests. I'd loaded in a fresh tape, and was determined not to use all of it on my foot. Instead, I shot the river and the canoes ahead.

They were always ahead. Bono's job, was, as Phillip's had been on the game hikes, to bring up the rear, which meant he couldn't pass anyone. And some of the paddlers were slow. Very slow. The other husband, Simon, was remarkably bad. He kept ramming his canoe into the bank. In the canoe lesson, I'd thought he was practicing. Now it seemed he had an affinity for it. All he had to do was drift anywhere near the bank and his canoe would find it.

That slowed him down immensely, created a wide gap between them and group ahead. As this stretched out to the length of a football field, Bono took action. "Go fast," he counseled.

It turned out the way to go fast, once he managed to impart it — his English was not particularly good, unless he, like Duke, took pains to hide it — was for Simon to paddle very fast on alternating sides of the canoe and Trish to paddle very fast on the side near the bank, in order to attempt to overcome his natural attraction to it.

This method worked to some degree, and

I figured that if this was the time for Trish to paddle, it was also an opportunity for me. I grabbed up my paddle and got in a few quick strokes before Bono said, "No, no."

Even without me paddling, Bono was having a hard time not passing Simon and Trish. Finally he got them caught up to the pack. Trish put her paddle away, relieving me of the humiliation of not paddling while she did. Not that anyone could see me, unless they turned fully around in their canoe.

I'd just had that thought when Victoria dropped her paddle. The young hero Keith was up ahead showing off some stroke or other, and didn't even see.

Stanley and Bono to the rescue. Or rather Bono to the rescue. He skillfully managed to maneuver his canoe and come up on the paddle so that it was just out of my reach, and floated into his. He scooped it out of the river with one hand, then zoomed up on Victoria's boat and presented it with a flourish.

I sat in the bow trying not to look foolish.

The cup of my ignominy was full.

Moments later, all that was forgotten as we rounded a bend in the river to an area where grass was lush and animals abounded.

There were four elephants on the left bank, a baby, two females, and a male. Not that I peeked at their privates. I knew from the shape of their heads. Female elephants have more pronounced heads than male elephants. I'm sure Alice thinks it's because they have more brains.

The elephants had come down to the river to drink, to bathe, to cool off, or do whatever elephants do. They paid absolutely no attention to our canoes. Apparently we didn't present any threat.

More elephants appeared on the right bank, which we were closer to. I hoped Simon and Trish wouldn't run into them. It didn't seem likely. They were trying to stay with the other canoes, which were giving the elephants a wide berth.

Then we were past them and into another stretch of the river where the banks were too steep to provide easy access. An impala appeared on the bank, didn't seem impressed, and trotted away.

The river widened and the banks became a gentle slope. Up ahead, Clemson was pointing to the left bank. I raised my binoculars to look. Couldn't see anything. The bank was just a bank.

No, it wasn't. Camouflaged against the sand was a crocodile. It appeared to be sleeping, but I wouldn't have bet my life on it. Now that I spotted it, I saw more lying on the bank. One was even moving, sliding into the water. How big was it? Ten, fifteen feet? It didn't matter. It was certainly big enough to do the job. I shuddered involuntarily.

Comforted myself with the thought that Clemson wouldn't be doing this if it was dangerous.

Wrong again.

33
At Long Last, Lion

The crocodile didn't eat us, nor did any of the other crocodiles we encountered lying on the banks of the river. There were dozens of them, eight or ten at a time, sunning themselves on the shore and occasionally slipping into the water.

I wondered what they ate. I know: anything they felt like. I heard tell of the wildebeest migration where thousands would come across and the crocodiles could hang out and pick and choose. That wasn't happening here. I suppose a few zebras or impalas occasionally decided to cross, but surely that couldn't feed this multitude of crocs. I would have thought tourist was a popular entrée. But the crocodiles showed no interest. Maybe we just tasted bad. Anyway, they became a familiar enough sight that no one panicked when they appeared, even Annabel who panicked when the sun rose.

That wasn't all we saw, of course. There were more elephants, occasional zebras, none of whom wanted to cross. That was good. Much as I wanted to film some action, having a zebra torn apart by a hungry croc was not my idea of must-see TV. I wouldn't have minded if a crocodile had chased them away from the bank, however. A little action without carnage.

We came around a bend in the river where the banks were steep and the crocs were gone. The people in the canoes up ahead were pointing at the right bank. Bono and I were mired behind Simon and Trish, who, even without bumping the bank, had fallen far behind.

Instead of spurring them into action, Bono raised his finger to his lips and said, "Shhh!" and motioned them to paddle quietly up to the others. He did so by making a face, wide-eyed and teeth bright, and miming dipping his paddle silently into the water in an exaggerated caricature of a person attempting to be quiet. It was remarkable. Even sitting down in the canoe, he looked like someone sneaking into the house at midnight.

The canoes paddled silently after the others and I suddenly saw it. There, standing on the bank, was a lion. A daddy lion, as I used to tell Tommie at the Bronx Zoo. A male lion, with a mane, the King of Beasts. There he stood, calm, unruffled, surveying the terrain.

We paddled up to the other canoes. They were together, side by side, facing the lion. Each person was holding on to the adjacent canoe. Bono and I fell in line next to Simon and Trish. I grabbed their canoe with one hand, my binoculars with the other.

He was sensational. Proud, regal. His eyes swept over us, unimpressed, the king bored with his lowly subjects. That reminded me, Alice would want an action shot. I dropped the binoculars, grabbed the camera. Used my left hand, which was still holding the canoe, to help slip my right hand under the strap. I flipped the screen out, switched the camera on.

By the time I raised it and hit RECORD, the lion had turned and walked away from the river. The bank was high enough and steep enough that he was quickly out of sight.

"Okay," Clemson whispered to the group. "Let's see where he goes." Beckoning for us to follow, he paddled his canoe to shore and beached it on the bank.

Alice, in the bow of his canoe, turned and gave him an are-you-kidding-me? look.

Clemson was already up and crowding her out of the canoe. "Come on, come on. Let's see!"

Alice hopped out of the canoe. Clemson had rammed it far enough up the bank that her footing was dry. He hopped out behind her, gestured to the others to follow. He tugged the bow of the librarians' canoe up on the shore, gave them a hand getting out.

Keith was already out of his canoe, herding Jason in front of him so he could help Victoria and Annabel while Clemson helped Simon and Trish.

Bono, like Clemson, expertly ran the canoe far enough up the bank that I could step out with no problem.

In seconds we were all assembled at the foot of the bank.

Alice voiced the general opinion. "Are you nuts?" she said. "There's a lion up there."

"I thought you wanted to see one," Clemson said.

"From the jeep," Annabel said. "We wanted to see one from the jeep."

"Nonsense," Clemson said. "It's a walking safari. We could have found a lion any time. It was disappointing that we didn't, but, hey, we got lucky. We found a lion now. Let's see if he's still here."

Without waiting for more objections, he

251

turned and scrambled up the bank.

We stared at him, dumbfounded.

"Come on, come on," he said. "This is your chance."

It was Keith's chance to impress Victoria by being brave, and he scrambled up the hill behind. Others followed. I snapped the video camera on, took a shot of this happening. Not so much to delay my own ascent of the hill as to document the event. Alice started climbing. I caught a shot of her and followed.

There we all were, in a line, just below the crest of the bank. Was the lion still there? The only way to tell was by sticking your head up. That seemed an awfully poor option. It would either be disappointing, or bring you face-to-face with a lion.

That didn't stop Clemson. He stuck his head up over the top of the bank and said, "He's gone."

We looked then, some more hesitantly than others, as if Clemson were capable of playing a practical joke, which I wouldn't have put past him. But it was true. The lion was gone.

"Come on, let's see where he went," Clemson said. He climbed up onto the bank and looked back, surprised that no one was with him. We all looked up with somewhat bemused faces. This time no one asked him if he was crazy. We knew the answer.

Clemson waved his hand. "Come on, come on, before he gets away."

Somehow a lion getting away from me is a concept I had never imagined. I mean, it's not as if we were going to stop him. I certainly hoped we weren't. The only way I could think of was to shoot him or let him eat Bono.

Clemson prevailed through the strength of his personality. On the river, without guides and rangers to inhibit him, he had blossomed into Steve Irwin, Crocodile Hunter, only armed and dangerous with none of the reserve. The only reassuring thought, and there weren't many, was if he hadn't gotten himself killed by now, he probably wouldn't get *me* killed.

"Okay," Clemson said. "This is just another walking safari. Single file, follow me, keep ahead of Bono bringing up the rear."

We set off with Clemson in the lead, Alice right behind. No surprise there. Alice always was the smartest person in the room. In case of a lion, she wanted to be right behind the man with the gun.

The two librarians fell in next, then Victoria and Annabel. A great deal of negotiation preceded this, with Victoria suggesting it would be safer in the middle of the line than near the end. I doubt if that was what swayed Annabel. She just didn't want to be left alone.

Close on their heels were Keith and Jason, followed by Simon and Trish.

I brought up the rear, just ahead of Bono.

Clemson found the lion's tracks, leading away from the river. We followed them until they disappeared in the thicker vegetation. Clemson pushed ahead, undeterred, through a narrow path in the brush.

It dawned on me we might actually find the lion. I know, I know, that was the whole point. It was just that the danger of what we were doing had overshadowed the goal. But, I realized, the prospect of finding a lion was exciting as hell.

I swung my backpack off my shoulders, dug out the video camera again. If we found it, I was going to film it.

Optimally, I wanted to film the actual moment of us finding it. That would mean running the camera for a while, but if I could shoot forty-five minutes of my leg, I could certainly shoot a few minutes of us creeping through the underbrush. I flipped out the screen, switched the camera on.

Since we were walking in a straight line, all I could get was Trish. When the path widened up into a little clearing, I took two steps to the right and got an angle on the group. I zoomed in on Alice and Clemson in the lead.

Two things happened just then. Bono told me to get back in line, and Clemson began to run ahead, waving his hand, "Come on! Come on!"

No one wanted to let the man with the rifle get away. We all ran with him.

And there we were, clomping through the underbrush, bouncing up and down the way you do when you're out of shape and not used to running over rugged terrain wearing a backpack.

Having no idea what had impelled this burst of speed, I kept the camera rolling. I managed to zoom back to wide angle in case we came up on anything to see.

After about a hundred yards I was panting and wishing it would end. It didn't, of course. We went down a small arroyo and up the other side to the crest of a hill, which looked like a good vantage point if anyone wanted to spot a lion. Instead, Clemson led us down the other side into the bush. Whereupon he stopped, listened, looked around. Studied the ground for prints. He found some that petered out again. I know because Bono pointed them out to me as we passed. We'd been going the right way, it was just that a lion was faster than a bunch of middle-aged tourists, even when they jog.

I wondered how far we were from the canoes. It was hard to tell, since we'd been running. We wouldn't be running back. Even if I had to read Clemson the riot act. The only way we'd be running back was if a lion were chasing us.

At the moment we were picking our way down the path, slowly, carefully, so as not to miss a thing. You can't see everything because the brush is thick, and there are too many directions to watch. It's the only way I can account for what happened.

Because Clemson went first, of course, with everyone following him. And no one saw a thing.

Except Trish.

Trish stopped dead. Her face was electric. Her eyes were wide and her mouth gaped open in a terrified grin. She pointed to the side of the path in an exaggerated gesture, jabbing her finger in front of her face.

I looked, and my mouth fell open.

The lion was right there. In the bush. Sitting up. Looking at us. Next to the path. Not six feet away.

I did my best Trish impression, looked to Bono.

"Walk," Bono said calmly.

He didn't have to tell me twice, though he did. Actually he told me three times. "Walk. Walk away."

It seemed like good advice. Bono wasn't armed, and I'm sure he wanted to put as much distance between him and the lion as possible.

Bono whistled and Clemson turned. Bono made there's-a-lion signals. Clemson nodded, picked up the pace. He had been walking slowly, searching the brush. How he had missed the lion I had no idea. Now he walked right along, at the same time putting his hands out, palms down, enjoining us not run or do anything else to attract attention. He walked through the brush, turned right, headed up a hill. At the top he turned back to the right.

I knew what he was doing. He was circling back on the lion.

He stopped on the crest of the hill overlooking the bush where it had been, raised his binoculars, and looked.

"Which bush?" he said.

Trish pointed mutely. She probably didn't trust herself to speak.

Clemson focused in on the bush. "There he is. See him?"

I grabbed my binoculars, couldn't see him at all.

"See him?" I asked Alice.

"Yeah," Alice said. "You can just see the mane. Oh! There he goes!"

The lion ran off into the bush. At least that's what they told me. I never saw a thing.

We spent a few minutes studying the bush, to no avail. The lion was gone.

Great.

We finally saw a lion.

It scared me to death.

And I didn't get it on film.

34
TRISH FACE

It was the talk of lunch. Trish's encounter with the lion. Someone would make what came to be known as the Trish face, and we would all crack up. Luckily, now that it was over, Trish found it pretty funny too.

At first Simon, to his credit, was ready to leap to her defense, should the need arise. But as he realized she was taking it well, he relaxed and we all had fun.

Lunch was on a bank overlooking the river. Not *that* bank. We got back in the canoes and paddled a good way downstream before docking again.

"We want to *have* lunch, we don't want to *be* lunch," Clemson said, a twinkle in his eye. Clemson was in his element, having the time of his life.

Lunch was sandwiches and soft drinks set out on a makeshift table about the size of a TV tray which Bono had brought along in our canoe. There was also sliced fruit. It was not a sumptuous repast, but it was ten times better than dinner the night before. Being on the river made all the difference in the world.

And having just seen a lion.

"I don't know how I missed it," Simon said. "I was right in front of her. I just walked by and, arrrrh!" He made a Trish face, having come to the realization that it was all right to do so.

We all laughed, including Trish, but hers was somewhat strained. By then she must have been wondering how long people were going to tease her.

I'd have bet on quite a while. The Trish face was amazingly addictive.

It was time to float a trial balloon.

"A shame Alice never got to see it," I said.

That killed the mood. There was an awkward silence.

I looked over at Clemson. He seemed to approve, but he wasn't jumping in.

"You think she'd have made a Trish face?" Trish said. She made one, and we all laughed again, and the moment had passed.

So. No one wanted to talk about it. I wondered if that was significant, or if the subject was just a natural downer. The latter seemed likely. My remark might have made the killer uneasy, but it was lost in the shuffle because everyone was.

My task, finding a killer who likely wasn't there, wasn't going to be easy.

At least Clemson would see that I had taken a stab at it.

After lunch Bono walked into the brush, nothing ate him, and we were able to mark our territory.

We got back in our canoes, headed out on the river.

I started noticing pairs of eyes staring at me. At first I thought it was crocs. Then one yawned and I saw it was a hippo.

Clemson gave them a wide berth, sometimes crossing the river just to keep away from them. After his bravado with the lion, his healthy respect for the hippos made an impression.

We came to a spot where two legs of the river joined together, making it wider and faster.

"Okay," Clemson said. "We have to get to the other side. It's a strong current, and we have to paddle through it. Point your canoe a little upstream because you're going to get pushed back down. I'll go first, show you where to aim. In case you get in trouble, Bono will be bringing up the rear. So do what I do. Paddle a little upstream until you get caught by the current, then paddle like crazy for the other shore. Try to land as close to me as possible. If you land a little downstream, that's fine. If you go way downstream, it's not."

"We wouldn't go down there," one of the librarians said. I'm pretty sure it was Pam.

"You will if you get caught by the current. And you don't want to wind up there. See all the hippos? That would be very bad news."

"Are they really so dangerous?" Keith said.

"You'd be better off tangling with a crocodile."

"Wait a minute," Annabel said. "You're rowing us into a bunch of dangerous hippos?"

"Paddling," Victoria said. "He's *paddling* us into a bunch of dangerous hippos."

"It's not funny." Annabel was getting hysterical. "First a lion almost eats us, then this. The boy's dead, and Alice is dead, and who's next?"

"Annabel," Clemson said sharply. "Look at me."

She did. It was amazing the way he could pull focus.

"Was Daniel killed by an animal? No. Was Alice killed by an animal? No. No one was killed by an animal, and no one's going to be killed by an animal while I'm in charge.

Even if I have to shoot every hippo in the river. Victoria, you paddle right behind me. If you go off course, I've got you."

"I'll be right behind you," Keith said. "Nothing to worry about."

The librarians nodded at each other. Neither looked particularly worried.

"What about me?" Trish said.

I could understand her concern. Her canoe had been off course all day.

"Bono will be right behind you," Clemson said. "There's nothing to worry about. When you hit the current, you paddle like crazy on the right side of the canoe. Okay, here we go."

Before anyone else could protest, he and Alice set off across the river.

We all followed with varying degrees of trepidation.

Halfway across, the current hit us. Victoria didn't do badly, and Keith and the librarians had no problems, but Trish and Simon immediately began losing ground.

Bono was right alongside, shouting encouragement. "Paddle! Paddle! Paddle! Don't paddle! Paddle! Paddle! Paddle!"

Paddle, paddle, paddle was for Trish and Simon, who, for the first time all day, were having trouble aiming their canoe at the bank. Don't paddle was for me, the nonessential personnel.

We reached the shore without incident. Simon and Trish were about thirty or forty yards downstream, still way shy of the hippos.

Under Clemson's guidance, we skirted the hippos and continued downstream. It was idyllic, if uneventful. Which shows how quickly one can get jaded. It was not as if we weren't seeing animals. There were hippos galore, none close enough to be threatening. They glided beneath the surface like submarines, just the twin periscopes of their eyes betraying their presence. Some watched us as we went by. None made a move in our direction.

And there were crocodiles, either sleeping or elaborately unimpressed by our presence. I wasn't fooled. I had no doubt if I hopped out of the canoe and began thrashing my legs, they'd be on me in a second.

There were elephants and an occasional zebra, even a water buffalo or two. Nothing to write home about. By now we were big game hunters, armed only with cameras but ready to take on even the wildest of beasts.

As we drifted down the river, my mind went back over the events of the day, trying to see if there was anything that would shed some light, however dim, on my appointed task. Nothing jumped out at me. Like Trish's lion. Which hadn't jumped out at her, just sat there in the bush, minding its own business, watching all the tourists go by, and inspiring the immortal Trish face.

I realized that Trish was one of the few people who'd alluded to the murders at all. And that was only because I'd brought it up, mentioned Alice. And no one said anything. There was just a silence. And Trish finally said I wonder if she would have made a Trish face. Skillfully diverting the conversation by dismissing it with a joke.

Was it significant that she had? She was tired of jokes about the Trish face, that was apparent. And here she was making one. Inviting ridicule again. Why would she have done that? Did she have something to hide?

Aside from her, the only one to mention the murders was Annabel. And she'd brought it up herself. Daniel had been killed, and Alice had been killed, and who was next? She'd dragged that remark in from left field just because she was scared about paddling through the current. That had to make her innocent, right? Or why would she have brought it up?

Unless it was an elaborate double-bluff. Which she didn't appear capable of. But then who knew what she was capable of?

She was a jealous, fearful, and possessive woman, always on the lookout for any threat to her sister, and not just of bodily harm.

Daniel was a handsome young stud. If he were making a play for Victoria, Annabel might have felt impelled to protect her virtue. And what if Alice had gotten an inkling? She'd been questioning the staff. Suppose they'd told her about Daniel's success with women. Tourist women in particular. It might have been enough to send Alice to Victoria. And Victoria, suspecting nothing, could have cast blame on her sister. Alice could have confronted Annabel with the truth, and Annabel could have been forced to act.

Or —

What if Victoria hadn't taken kindly to Daniel's advances? In the same way she'd been rebuffing Keith. And what if Daniel was persistent? Victoria had sneaked off to meet Daniel in his camp, just to give her sister a hard time. She'd rebuffed his advances, and he wouldn't take no for an answer. And she had to fight him off. And happened to pick up a stick.

And what if Alice had suspected? And questioned Annabel. Not for confirmation of Annabel's guilt, but to confirm her suspicions about Victoria. Annabel could have sprung into action to protect her sister.

That would mean two separate murderers, unforgivable in a mystery novel, possible in real life.

I drifted down the river, not paddling, lost in idle speculation.

35
River Camp

Around four-thirty we arrived at bush camp. It differed from our previous bush camp by being semi-permanent. Our Zambian bush camp was totally mobile. Had we stayed there longer and not done the canoe trip, we'd have taken hikes into the bush and the camp would have come with us. While we were hiking, the staff would have broken everything down, driven to the next site, pitched the tents, and dug a straight-drop toilet.

The Zimbabwean bush camp had permanent tents with individual toilets.

I was delighted to have my own toilet, until I tried it. It did not flush. On inspection, there seemed little likelihood of that ever happening. The hose supposedly bringing water up to the flushable tank above was so badly crushed and twisted, it was a wonder it was still connected. The chance of water flowing through was negligible. So the only way to flush the toilet was to scoop water out of one of our two sinks, canvas pouches on wooden frames which the staff filled with water for us to wash up in. That was in theory. In practice, one canvas pouch was ripped so all the water ran out. That left one sink-full of water to either wash your hands in or pour down the toilet to flush it.

I missed the straight-drop toilet.

I missed other things too. The tents were exactly like the ones in bush camp. Except, since they were never moved, they were never maintained. There were holes in the canvas, most of the ties were gone so it was impossible to keep the side flaps up, and the zipper on the netting was stuck open so mosquitoes were likely to get in and give me malaria no matter how much Malarone I took.

The tents, of course, were pitched along the river. It was beautiful in the setting sun. Alice got out the camera and began snapping shots, one of which I was sure would wind up as the screen saver on her computer.

Dinner was served on a square table big enough to seat us all. It was set out in the open by the campfire. There was also a table with coffee, liquor, and cold drinks.

Trish had bourbon, which I figured she needed after the lion. She drank it off fairly quickly, poured another. The librarians had gin and tonics, which they sipped decorously. Victoria had wine. So did Annabel, though she poured it grudgingly, as if unhappy to emulate her sister. Clemson, Keith, and Jason were having beer. I got the impression they'd be having more than one.

Dinner was served by the staff, who won our hearts by announcing fish, then lost them by serving it. The fish was whole, not filleted, burnt on the outside, raw on the inside. It had been gutted, but not well. It smelled vaguely like dried vomit. No one ate much, but no one complained. A lot of bread was consumed.

I wanted to bring up the murder, but there was no chance. Talk was all about what we'd seen on the river. Every now and then someone would make a Trish face, but the hysteria was over.

We were picking our way through some sort of bread pudding that appeared to have been made without bread when Clemson raised his hand and said "Shhh!"

I hadn't heard a thing, and I doubt if anyone else had either.

Clemson had his head up, scenting the wind. I wondered if he actually was. It was pitch dark and there was no sound.

Clemson raised his finger to his lips, stood up, and said "Come on."

It was like when he set off after the lion. No one wanted to be left behind.

I had my headlight around my neck. So did Alice. We'd slipped them on when we went to dinner because it was getting dark, but not dark enough to need them yet. Anyway, I could have put the light on, but I'd have rather been shot dead. Which was entirely likely. Clemson was armed and wouldn't be happy.

I joined the pack tiptoeing behind Clemson in the dark. For the most part we were quiet. There was one sharp, whispered, "Stop it!" from Victoria, probably indicating that Keith had gotten fresh, but that was it.

Clemson led us into an open meadow that sloped slightly uphill away from the river. Halfway through the field he stopped and his flashlight clicked on. It was aimed at the ground and he was shielding the beam with his fingers.

All that could be seen were a hundred pairs of eyes gleaming in the darkness.

Annabel shrieked in terror.

And the eyes turned in our direction.

Clemson raised the flashlight.

In the meadow, staring at us, was an entire

herd of water buffalo, black horned creatures, each the size of a Mack truck, any one of which was capable of goring us and trampling us into the ground.

If Clemson had meant to reassure Annabel by revealing the source of her fright, he had badly miscalculated. She went further over the edge, and the level of her shrieks increased exponentially. The only way Clemson could have shut her up was to shoot her.

Victoria saved the day, leaping in front of her sister, a human shield, protecting her while calming her down with gentle ridicule.

"Come on," Clemson whispered. "No one run. Walk away quietly. I'm going to douse the light."

He did. It seemed even darker than before, now that our eyes had adjusted to the light.

This precipitated a fresh squeal from Annabel, but she quickly muffled it, and we managed to sneak back to the campfire.

"How long have they been there?" Alice wanted to know.

"Since the end of dinner," Clemson said.

"How do you know?" I asked.

"I heard them coming."

I hadn't heard a thing. Of course, our ears weren't trained for it, but still it was pretty impressive.

"Well," Clemson said, "it's been a long day, and tomorrow will be even longer, so you probably want to get to sleep."

"Sleep?" Annabel said. "How can we sleep with those animals out there? We're apt to be trampled in our beds."

"Water buffalo aren't interested in tents," Clemson said. "They can't eat them, so they just go around them. It's perfectly safe."

"What do you mean, tomorrow will be longer?" Simon said.

I could understand his concern. Trish's husband had not had an easy time paddling.

"Today we got a late start because we had to have a lesson. Now you know how to paddle." Clemson looked at Simon dubiously. "More or less. Anyway, you're as good as you're going to get, so there's nothing to do but throw you in the stream."

I could have paddled Trish, and let Simon go with Bono. Prudence kept me from suggesting it. Alice would never let me hear the end of it, fancying myself the young hero, leaping into the breach and rescuing the fair Trish. Her husband couldn't be too pleased either.

We all took Clemson's advice and headed back to our tents. I asked the staff men to fill our sink, so we could flush the toilet.

It was nice that the staff were all Zimbabwean and could not have figured in Daniel's death, so I didn't have to watch them closely for signs of guilt.

Alice and I washed up, brushed our teeth, got into bed.

The cot was in worse repair than the ones in bush camp. I had a feeling that if I lifted the mattress up, some of the springs would be missing.

It didn't matter. Clemson was right. The events of the day had been exhausting. It wouldn't take much to get to sleep.

As I drifted off, one image haunted me.

It wasn't the hundreds of eyes gleaming in the dark. Or the close herd of water buffalo that appeared when he clicked on the light.

It was the sight of Victoria, leaping in front of her sister to calm her down.

Clearly, despite all protestations to the contrary, Victoria actually loved her sister, and would do anything to protect her.

Including murder?

36
HIGH WIND

I woke up and the wind was blowing. No one realized the significance until Clemson brought it up at breakfast, which that morning was eggs and oatmeal and the ever-popular campfire toast. We had all taken our portions and were sitting around the big table when Clemson dropped the bomb.

"If the wind keeps up, we can't go out on the river."

The announcement was greeted with shock and surprise.

"Why not?" Pam wanted to know. She was the librarian who had stood in line with me outside the shower, and I'd figured out her name by remembering she had referred to the other librarian as Edith, making her Pam. A small victory, but mine own. I hadn't solved the murder, but I had named the librarians.

"It's too rough to paddle," Clemson said. "It would be dangerous."

I took that seriously. Lots of things were dangerous, and Clemson did them anyway.

"What if it dies down?" Alice said.

"If it dies down, we go. If it's like this, we don't. Look at those whitecaps. As long as the river's like that, it's not safe."

"It looks okay to me," Keith said. It was a typical Keith remark, macho, arrogant, and stupid. I was delighted to see that no one paid any attention.

"So what do we do instead?" Edith said. I nailed the name easily, didn't even have to think about it.

"We have a game hike," Clemson said.

There were universal groans.

"Yes, I know, that's what you've been doing, and you came here to do something different. Trust me, it will be different."

"How?" Simon wanted to know. Freed from paddling, he was the only one who seemed happy to hike.

"For one thing, I'll be leading it. For another, we'll all walk together. No need to split into groups."

"How come we can do that here?"

"Because we don't have a ranger, so we don't have to play by their rules. Believe me, we'll have fun. We'll set out here, hike around, be back between eleven and twelve. If the wind's died down, we'll be on the river after lunch. So, go back to your tents, get what you need out of your river bag, pack your backpack. You take water, sunscreen, hat, binoculars, camera if you want one. Trust me, you'll want one."

"How do you know?" Alice said.

"Because I've been here before. Okay, meet back here in twenty minutes."

I followed Alice back to the tent.

"You know, there's a lot of things you could do in twenty minutes," I said.

Alice ignored the remark, began packing her backpack. Nearly everything in her river bag came out and went in. The only thing she didn't need was the waterproof bag for her camera, her second line of defense against getting it wet.

I didn't really want to bring the movie camera. My backpack was heavy enough with just the water, particularly if Clemson started running again. But if I didn't, we'd see something special and Alice would never forgive me.

I tugged the camera out of the river bag, put it in the backpack. That was basically it. I didn't take sunscreen. Alice burns, but I tan, and when I use sunscreen I always get the damn stuff in my eyes and wind up squinting all day. My binoculars I wore in the harness. My hat I wore on my head. The water bottle I had to pick up off the table when we left.

I took out the camera, checked the battery to see if I'd accidentally left it on and run the damn thing down. Not that there was anything I could do about it. I didn't have another battery, and there was no time to charge it. But if it was dead, I could leave it behind.

It was fully charged. Stanley Hastings Productions was in business.

I went out, retrieved our water bottles, joined the group.

"Oh, that's what I forgot," Simon said. "We need our water bottles."

"Oh," Trish said.

"Don't worry, I'll get them," he said, and headed for the table.

I felt his pain. Unsuccessful at paddling, the poor man was trying to get back in her good graces by being useful retrieving water.

"Okay," Clemson said. "Same drill as before. Single file, follow me, keep up, Bono will bring up the rear.

He set off into the bush.

Annabel was right on his heels. She must have learned the concept that sticking with him was safest. She aced Alice out. It was no contest. She stood next to him during

278

the briefing, was glued to him when he took off.

Naturally Victoria took off with her, which made Keith third and Jason fourth. The librarians came next, followed by Simon and Trish, who didn't want to be last. That honor was left for me and Alice.

I was bummed out. I had planned on jumping in behind Alice and being in the front of the line for once, instead of on the end. But, oh no, there I was, right in front of Bono.

I wondered if that meant Alice would be the one to walk by the lion.

We left camp through the water buffalo meadow. There was not a water buffalo to be seen. I was glad.

Clemson turned left, went down what was almost a path into another clearing, and there was an elephant. No one was alarmed. Those with cameras at the ready began snapping shots. Those without dug in their backpacks for theirs. I dug in mine, whipped out the movie camera, snapped it on.

We were on the edge of the clearing. The elephant was in the middle. His head swung toward us.

"Okay," Clemson said. "Let's all back up toward that tree."

He moved slowly backward to do so. We

followed suit. There was a mound of dirt around the tree, making it impossible to reach the trunk. Clemson leaned up against it, half sitting, half standing. We lined up next to him, supported ourselves with the dirt, raised our cameras.

"Okay," Clemson said. "How many of you have been up close with an elephant?"

I don't know why he asked us that. The first camp had been full of elephants. We'd all had close encounters, most of us more than one. Which is why we weren't panicking.

"Stay calm. Don't move," Clemson said.

The elephant began slowly lumbering toward us. I put the camera on record, watched through the viewfinder.

The elephant got bigger, and bigger, and bigger.

It charged!

Oh, my god!

It was ready for its close-up and I wasn't.

I felt an amazing adrenaline rush of blind fear. I flinched, my feet slipped in the dirt, I slid sideways and plunked down on my back, the camera pointing every which way except at the elephant. I braced my elbows into the dirt mound and looked up.

The elephant had stopped. He was close, as Clemson had said, but he wasn't in our laps. His tusks weren't in anyone's chest, and his feet weren't on anyone's toes. Basically a win-win.

"You might want to get up," Clemson said. "You're lying in a termite mound."

"What?"

"That's what the big mound of dirt is." Clemson grinned. "You know the expression ants in your pants?"

I looked around and everyone was laughing. Of course they were. I looked damn silly.

Oh!

I suddenly realized that I'd just become Trish.

I wondered if I'd made a Stanley face.

37
GAME DRIVE, CLEMSON STYLE

I was wrong on all counts. No one was laughing at me. They were laughing at themselves, nervous relieved laughter at the various degrees of panic they had experienced when the elephant charged.

"Ralphie's very inquisitive," Clemson explained as we sat around eating lunch. We were back in camp after a relatively uneventful hike. Don't get me wrong, we saw zebras, warthogs, giraffes, and impalas, and even tracked but never saw a smaller cat of some sort, but after the elephant everything seemed tame.

"You know this elephant?" Alice said.

"That's Ralphie. He often hangs out here."

"You let him scare us to death," Annabel said.

"You were never in any danger."

"You knew that. We didn't."

"Would it have been as much fun if you

had?" Clemson asked.

"Fun, schmun," Victoria said. "I nearly peed in my pants."

Everyone laughed except Keith, who seemed to find the image disturbing, humanizing his goddess. How did he think she marked her territory, with little flags?

He stomped off to the river, was back moments later. "The wind's died down," he said. "The river looks calm."

The upper branches of the trees punctuated his statement by swaying ominously.

"Sorry," Clemson said. "I don't think we'll get on the river today."

That pleased no one but Simon. And I think Trish was a little relieved too.

"Oh, come on," Keith said. "We paid good money for this."

"Yes, you did," Clemson said. "But I can't guarantee good weather. Any more than I can guarantee you'll see a lion. We've had very good weather, and we've not only seen a lion, but a lion has seen us. You're getting your money's worth. It may not be exactly according to schedule, but schedules are subject to change. You gotta be flexible. Remember we came here a day early. If we want to spend an extra day on the river to make sure we get in the canoes, we can do it."

"And then we lose a day on the other end," Keith said. "What's on the schedule that we're going to lose?"

Clemson smiled slightly. "A hike and a game drive. The walk this morning was different, wasn't it? The game drive will be different too."

The game drive was just like every other game drive we'd been on, except Clemson was driving.

I was in Clemson's jeep. I made sure of that, skipping a trip to the unflushable toilet and heading straight for the jeep after lunch. Turned out I needn't have bothered. We were *all* in Clemson's jeep. Three in each seat, and one up front with him. Bono stayed behind. For the game drive, Clemson was driver, guide, spotter, and ranger. For him, it didn't seem unreasonable.

Keith was torn between riding shotgun with Clemson and sitting next to Victoria. The librarian named Pam solved the problem for him by climbing into the front seat with Victoria and Annabel. That left one librarian for me and Alice, but she opted for Trish and Simon. That left the moody, sullen Jason, next to Keith my least favorite traveling companion. He climbed in next to me. Alice, of course, had the side seat for her camera, so I was stuck in the middle.

Sullen tourists to the left of me, wives to the right, here I am stuck in the middle with you.

I couldn't think of a single thing I wanted to say to Jason. That seemed to suit him just fine. He sat, sipped his water, fidgeted with his ring. I wondered if it was a wedding ring. If so, I wondered if he'd killed his wife.

All aboard, we took off in the jeep in quest of adventure. We found none. The dirt road we were bumping along wasn't much, but it was definitely a road. We occasionally passed vehicles heading in the other direction. I wondered if they knew something.

We saw a few animals, but nothing worth stopping for.

After a while, Alice put her camera in her lap. She leaned across me to Jason.

"First time in Africa?"

He didn't hear her. At least he didn't believe she was talking to him. He looked up, saw that she was. "What?"

"Is it your first time on safari?"

"Uh-huh."

"Us too. We've never been anywhere. It something I've always wanted to do."

He smiled vaguely, nodded, said nothing.

"You travel much?" Alice said.

"Just for my job."

"Oh? What do you do?"

I got the impression he was torn between answering the question and telling her to go to hell.

"I work for an insurance company."

"You sell insurance?"

"I hate to say that. People are afraid I'll make a pitch."

"Your secret's safe with us," Alice said.

He went back to staring moodily out of the side of the jeep. He hadn't asked Alice what she did. He was either rude, or just didn't want to talk. Probably both.

It was getting on and we hadn't seen anything. I wondered if Keith was giving Clemson a hard time. I couldn't hear what he was saying from the back seat. I could hear Clemson when he made a pronouncement, of which there had been damn few, but I couldn't tell if Keith was whining. If so, it must have taken great forbearance for Clemson not to draw his revolver and shoot him in the head.

I realized I had to mark my territory. "Hey, Clemson," I called. "I'd like to own some of this land. You think I could stake it out?"

Clemson pulled up by the side of the road. "Let me check the bush."

He did, found nothing. I'd have been

surprised if he had. We hadn't found anything all afternoon.

I got out, marked my territory, came back
to find a line of fellow markers. I climbed
up over Alice.

"Got the hand sanitizer?"

"Uh-huh." She dug in her backpack. "Just
a drop. Here, I'll do it for you."

I held out my palms. She squeezed the
barest trace of hand sanitizer out of the
plastic bottle. I rubbed my hands together,
became socially acceptable again.

We drove on, saw nothing.

About ten minutes later, Clemson stopped
the jeep and got out. That was weird. We'd
just had a pit stop. What was he doing?

Clemson walked around to the front of
the jeep, knelt down, examined the road.
He raised his binoculars, looked off to the
left.

I raised my binoculars, tried to see what
he was looking at. I didn't see anything. I
was not surprised. I'm an expert at seeing
nothing.

Clemson got back in the jeep, turned
around. "Hang on, kids, it's gonna be a
bumpy ride."

With that he jerked the wheel to the left
and drove off the road.

It was a bumpy ride, all right. Branches

were not whipping at us and small saplings were not being plowed underneath the jeep, but as far as bumps went it was everything he'd advertised.

I found myself clinging to the metal handrail across the back of the seat. Alice was cradling her camera like a newborn child, and jouncing up and down.

Up front people were bouncing in all directions, at least as far as they could go without bumping into someone. Which wasn't far, the jeep being crowded as it was. Keith must have been cursing himself for not ousting the librarian. If he had, Victoria would have been falling all over him.

The field we were bouncing through was pretty wide open. There was a tree line at the far side. I couldn't imagine hanging on like this for that long. About a hundred yards from the trees, Clemson stopped, raised his binoculars, and said, "Look!"

There was a single tree somewhat out in the open, and that seemed to be what Clemson was looking at.

I scanned the tree with my binoculars. Saw nothing in the branches, nothing in the leaves. Moved down the trunk.

And there at the bottom!

Could it be?

Were those ears?

Yes, they were! And a tawny feline face!

"Leopard?" Edith said.

She'd spotted it just before me, and I'd missed another chance to be wrong.

"Cheetah," Clemson said. "A mother and her cubs."

Cubs!

The buzzword raced through the jeep.

Cubs!

I half expected Clemson to leap out of the jeep and lead us across the field. Instead, he inched the jeep forward. We were still bumping along, just not at teeth-rattling velocity.

Clemson drove up about as close as we could get, then went closer. Finally he pulled up and parked sideways to the tree. Luckily it was Alice's side, or she might have climbed over me.

At the base of the tree were a mother and three cubs. The mother was sitting up. It was her ears I'd seen. The cubs were big. Not as big as mommy, maybe three quarters of her size. I was disappointed. I'd been hoping for kittens.

Still, it was a mother cheetah and her cubs. Only they were sleeping. And showed no signs of waking up.

That didn't stop the cameras. There came a staccato burst of click, click, clicks as photographers fired off shot after shot like machine guns. Even I whipped out the video camera and shot mommy and the cubs. About a minute of them sleeping was all I could handle, even with zooming and panning and pulling back to include a piece of the jeep in the foreground, which was all I could do without getting out and walking around. I wondered if we would.

We didn't. Even after the cameras stopped shooting. We just sat there. Watched the sleeping cubs.

"What are we doing?" Keith wanted to know.

"Waiting," Clemson said.

That we were. A few minutes later we were still waiting, the cheetahs were still sleeping, and I was beginning to feel like a man trapped in a shaggy-cat story.

Mommy got up, yawned, stretched, walked over to the cubs, and lay down again.

Audible groans rippled through the jeep.

"Why can't we wake them up?" Keith said.

Clemson shook his head. "We're just observers. We can't interfere."

"With what?"

"Nature. It has to take its course."

"Why?" Keith demanded. "What difference could it possibly make whether that cheetah is awake or asleep right now?"

"It'll make a difference to whatever it kills

because it wakes up angry and hungry."

"Isn't it going to kill something anyway?"

"Yes, but it should be her choice and not ours."

"Can we go?" Keith whined.

"Oh, let's have a snack first," Clemson said. He reached in a storage compartment, pulled out a cellophane bag. "Who wants some chips?"

They weren't potato chips. They were banana chips, a safari snack staple. They were as crisp as potato chips, but not as salty and a little thicker. We passed the bag around, and I took a few. Alice eyed me, counting the calories.

"Anything to drink?" Victoria said.

Clemson hopped out of the jeep, retrieved a cooler of soda and water out of the back. This pleased everyone but Keith, who was in a foul mood, probably because he wasn't sitting next to Victoria. "How come you can get out of the jeep and we can't?" he demanded.

Clemson smiled. "Because I have a rifle and a handgun and a hunting knife the size of a machete." He pulled the knife out of the sheath on his belt, held it in front of Keith's face. There was nothing overtly hostile in the gesture, but it got the point across. Keith shut up.

We drank the soda and nibbled the chips, pretended we weren't tired of watching sleeping cubs.

Mommy's head came up. I figured she was going to move another three feet and lie down again.

"Photo op," Keith said sarcastically.

Clemson stifled him. "Shhh! Look!"

I didn't know why he said that. We all were.

Then I realized he wasn't looking at the cheetah. He was looking behind her and off to the left.

Then I saw it.

An impala, standing in the clearing, looking around.

Mommy got up. Began to creep in that direction. Keeping low to the ground, out of its line of vision. She didn't creep straight at the impala. She crept off to the left, until she had a bush lined up between it and her. She crept slowly, quietly up behind the bush. Lay down. Inched up until she was peering out.

The impala, unaware of the danger, continued to nibble on leaves.

I had switched on the video camera the minute mommy got up, filmed her long stalk, what I could see of it in the tall grass. I zoomed in close on her lying under the bush. Pulled back to include the impala. They were both too small in the shot. I zoomed in on the impala, panned back to her.

She was moving! Slowly, very slowly, she had gone into a crouch, taken a step forward. And another. And another. And suddenly she was creeping along the ground, faster and faster, until —

She took off! And just like that she was gone, racing full-tilt after the frightened impala.

The jeep roared to life.

"Hang on!" Clemson shouted.

This time he really meant it. Clemson did his best cheetah impression, flying though the long grass as if his next meal depended on it. This time we really *were* snapping small saplings, and this time we really *did* have to hold on, or risk the very real possibility of being thrown from the jeep.

Mommy cheetah was not in sight. Nor was the impala. But my camera was still rolling lest they appear. Did I just say lest? That shows how excited I was. I couldn't even talk English, even bad, stilted, archaic English, and incorrect too. I don't mean lest. I mean in case. And —

Oh, my god! Did we just lose Trish!

We hadn't. She'd merely been thrown

sideways and disappeared behind her seat. She emerged unscathed, joined the throng of fearless impala hunters.

I don't know how long it lasted. It seemed forever, but was probably not more than a minute. The camera would tell me later.

And suddenly, there they were. The cheetah and the impala. They were on the ground. Mommy had it by the throat. It was dead. That was quick work. And a relief too. I didn't really want to see her kill it.

I had no sooner had that thought when it kicked. Not much, maybe just a reflex action. No, it kicked again, stronger this time. Mommy shifted her hold on its throat.

Cameras were clicking furiously. That reminded me I was holding mine. Realized I was focused on the scene. Did I really want to film this? Should I turn the camera off?

I didn't. I kept the camera on. I don't think I consciously considered being ridiculed as a wimp. At least not till later.

Mommy stood up, began dragging the impala through the tall grass.

"What's she doing?" Victoria asked.

Clemson turned in his seat. "Bringing it back to the cubs."

"But it's still alive."

"She's a good mommy. She wants the

cubs to finish it off. She's teaching them to kill prey."

Good lord. That's not how I would have thought of a good mommy, but it made perfect sense. And I kept the camera rolling, filmed the good mommy dragging the still-breathing impala through the bush.

Mommy didn't have to drag it far. The cubs had woken up and followed. She dragged it into a little clearing, assured herself it wasn't going to get up and run away, which it certainly wasn't. She let go of the neck and left it for the cubs.

They tried it, one at a time. Copied mommy. Grabbing the neck. Shaking and dragging.

They couldn't drag it. And they couldn't kill it. After all of that, one leg still kicked.

Finally mommy came back and finished the task. I could practically see her shaking her head. Boys, boys, when will you ever learn?

I wondered who'd eat first. Would Mommy take the cheetah's share, and leave it for the cubs to clean up? Or would she let her children eat? And, if so, would they be able to, or would she have to rip it open for them?

I was not to know. Having finished off the cheetah, Mommy walked over to a tree, lay down, and went to sleep.

So did the cubs.

I couldn't believe it. The cheetahs weren't dining. They were just stocking the refrigerator.

"They're not going to eat it?" Keith said. He sounded terribly disappointed, like some blood lust was going unsatisfied. I was not surprised. He was at the age it probably seemed like a video game. Blood Hunt, on PlayStation 3, or whatever number they were up to these days.

"They're tired," Clemson said. "You know how fast she went? She used up a lot of energy. They're set for dinner. They'll enjoy it better after a little nap."

"More waiting?" Keith said disgustedly.

I smiled, shook my head. Before Keith had been all, let's get out of here. Now he was like, how long will we have to stay?

"What?" Alice said.

I waved it away. "Tell you later."

38
SECOND NIGHT OF RIVER CAMP

Before dinner I wandered down by the river. I was restless, needed time to think. I tried to check out the wind. Were those whitecaps in the gathering dark? It was hard to tell. We'd been catching the wind all day, and things are relative. I hoped it would die down. After our eventful hike and drive, I could use a calm day drifting down the river.

I looked up to see one of the librarians wandering over to me. It was Pam. It took me a moment or two to name her. My first thought was still *a* librarian. Which was progress. It had been *a* Hells Angel.

"Looking at the river?" she said.

"Look calm enough to you?"

"I can't tell."

"Me either," I said. "I hope we go."

"You didn't enjoy today?"

"I did. I'm just not sure I can handle more enjoyment."

"The elephant charging was a little much."

"I'm not that keen at seeing animals torn limb from limb either."

"Oh, that's just nature. That's what predators do." After a pause she said, "Hard to believe one of us might be a killer."

I was surprised she'd brought it up. Most people had been avoiding the subject.

"Do you think it's one of us?"

She shrugged. "I don't know. I just can't picture one of the boys from bush camp killing Alice." She grimaced. "It must be hard for you, being married to an Alice."

"I doubt if she'd appreciate you saying being married to her must be hard."

"You know what I mean. You're the detective. Who do you think did it?"

"I have no idea. Do you?"

"Sure, but I'm not an expert."

"Me either. We're just people on a trip. If you have any ideas, I'd like to hear 'em."

Pam looked around. Lowered her voice. "Well, just between you and me, I think Alice suspected Jason."

"Really?"

"Well, I know she singled him out to talk to. And he's not *easy* to talk to."

"That's for sure. And she did?"

"Yes, she did."

"How do you know?"

"She told me."

"Oh?"

"She said he was very evasive. Like he had something to hide."

"Did you tell this to the police?"

"You mean to Duke? Of course not."

"Why not?"

"Well, it's hearsay, isn't it?"

"I don't know. If it's something the victim said, it might be part of the *res gestae.*"

"Oh, I forgot. You know these things."

I don't really. I knew the term from reading Perry Mason books, but I didn't know if it meant what I said it did, or if it even applied.

"Anyway, you weren't in court. Didn't he ask you what she said?"

"Yes, of course. And I told him what she said to *me.* I just didn't tell him what *she* said someone *else* said to *her.*"

That was a fine distinction. I don't think a lawyer could have split it better. I don't think the lawyer would have won the argument, but that's neither here nor there.

"What else did she tell you about Jason?"

"That was it. He was evasive and didn't want to talk. He didn't want to talk about the crime, and he didn't want to talk about where he came from and what he did."

"He sells insurance."

"That's what she said. Frankly, I just can't

see it. Would you buy insurance from that man? Anyway, he didn't want to talk about it. And insurance salesmen *always* want to talk about it. That's why they're insurance salesmen."

"He's on vacation."

"You wouldn't know it to look at him. I don't know why he came." She cocked her head. "So. Who do *you* think did it?"

"Colonel Mustard, in the billiard room, with the rhino rifle."

"You're not going to tell me, are you?"

"I wouldn't want to spoil the surprise."

"So you *do* have an idea."

"Not a clue."

Pam looked dissatisfied. I couldn't blame her. "Have it your way," she said. "But if you need someone to talk to, I'm available."

She squeezed out a forced, indulgent smile and grudgingly tore herself away.

I went back to staring moodily at the river.

"Hello, handsome."

I turned around to find Victoria smiling at me.

"You can drop the act. Your sister's not around."

"What do you mean?"

"You only flirt to make her crazy."

"Can't I just find you attractive?"

"You can't kid me. I know you've got a

thing for Keith."

She made a face. "Pul-lease!" she said. I could have sworn she was sixteen. "He is such a pest."

"Attentive, though."

"That's why he's a pest."

"That's what girls used to say in high school when they really liked someone."

"I'm not in high school."

"Me either."

"It's not like I've given him any encouragement."

"What more encouragement does a guy need? The indifferent act gets 'em every time."

"It's not an act. I don't like him. He's an arrogant creep. With his big Hollywood act."

"Hollywood?"

"Yeah, his whole are-you-an-actress-I-work-in-film act. Probably a gofer on some movie. If he works in film at all. Believe me, I know the type. He's a real pain."

"The guy he's traveling with is no picnic either."

"Jason? He's interesting."

"Because he's immune to your charm?"

"There's something about him."

Oh, my god, she had a thing for Jason. I felt a sinking feeling in my heart. Not that she liked someone else. That she liked *him.*

His sullen act really worked on women? I guess it did. They've always been attracted to the loner, the outcast, the fugitive, the rebel. Why did I waste my youth being affable?

"What does Jason do?" I asked.

"He didn't want to talk about it."

"Is he gay?"

"Of course he's not gay."

"Are you sure? I can't imagine any straight guy not being interested in you."

Alice came walking up.

Victoria said, "Oh, my god! It's your wife!" in an exaggerated stage whisper. "She caught us! Act natural!"

Alice laughed. "Are you stealing my husband?"

"I'm trying."

Alice shrugged. "Take him."

"Take my husband — please," I said.

"Stanley, she's too young for Henny Youngman."

Apparently she wasn't. "That's take my *wife* — please," Victoria said. "Take my husband — please would be Henri*etta* Youngman."

"Gotcha," I said, pointing at Alice. I shouldn't have. Siding with Victoria at Alice's expense was a bad husband move only slightly worse than selling mommy's firstborn child for crack.

Amazingly, Alice took it well. "You certainly did," she said. "But if you're going to take him, pay attention to the medical disclaimers: 'Persistent exposure may cause headaches, nausea, incredulity, frustration, uncontrollable rage, and divorce.' "

"Sounds like quite a catch," Victoria said.

"You have no idea."

I was pleased and surprised by Alice's tolerant reaction. It wasn't until we were on our way to dinner that it hit me. Alice wasn't angry about Victoria at all. Because Alice didn't see Victoria as a threat. Alice saw Victoria as a young girl, so far my junior that any flirtation she might indulge in would be the totally platonic ribbing of a sweet, elderly man. And Victoria could kid about it in front of Alice because she saw it that way too. Alice and Victoria were sharing a joke in which I was the butt of their humor.

That kind of spoiled my dinner.

39
EXTRADITION

"Stop by my tent," Clemson said after dinner.

"Where is it?"

"Follow the river."

"Huh?"

"Walk downstream. It's right there."

"I can go out by myself after dark?"

"Take a flashlight."

"What if there's lions?"

"Go around them."

At least I didn't ask him which way was downstream.

I went back to my tent, where Alice was getting ready for the shower. Our bathrooms didn't have individual showers, we had a communal one like back in bush camp. A line was already forming for it. I got my headlight, started out of the tent.

"You're not taking a shower?" Alice said.

"Clemson wants to see me."

"That can't be good."

"No kidding."

I had no problem finding Clemson's tent. I went in, found him sitting on his cot wearing nothing but a bath towel. Without his safari outfit he looked particularly pudgy and unathletic. It was hard to believe this was the same guy who went crashing through the underbrush chasing lions.

"I'm waiting for the shower," he explained. "The staff bathes last. Just like everything else. The tourists are always first. You didn't shower?"

"I skipped mine to make this meeting."

"Talk to the boys on your way out. They'll set you up."

"What did you want? Just a progress report? Because there really isn't any."

"That's not what I wanted to hear."

"I thought you thought it was one of Daniel's buddies."

"That would be nice." He grimaced. "I don't mean that. I mean it would be nice if it wasn't one of us."

"But you think it is?"

"I got the report from the lab."

"I thought you had it already. It was arsenic."

"That was the autopsy report. This is the lab analysis. They did tests to see how the arsenic was administered. They figured it was in the drinking water, which was how the staff would have done it. They filled the bottle. But it wasn't. And it wasn't in her food either."

"Where was it?"

"In her brandy."

"Brandy?"

"She had a flask of brandy. In her tent. She had a snort at night before going to bed. Which certainly mucks things up. The staff wouldn't have poisoned her flask. They didn't know she had it, and wouldn't have had time to look for it. If one of the staff wanted to poison her, he'd put it in the water bottle which was right in plain sight."

"That makes sense."

"The police think so too. So now it's very likely the killer was one of us."

"Why did it take so long to get the report?"

"I actually got it yesterday."

"Yesterday?"

"Yes."

"She was killed three days ago. That's still a long time."

Clemson said nothing.

"You got the report before," I said. "You just chose not to act on it."

"Absolutely not," he said. "I didn't get the report until we were on the river."

"You turned your cell phone off. That's why you didn't get the report. You turned your cell phone off until we were safely out of Zambia. That's why Duke was running after us in the parking lot. He'd probably just heard."

A voice outside the tent called, "Shower ready."

"You guys go first, then fill it up again," Clemson said.

"So now the U.S Embassy will step in," I said.

"What U.S. Embassy?"

"The Zambian one."

"We're not in Zambia."

"The Zimbabwean U.S. Embassy."

"But no one's been killed in Zimbabwe."

"Can't Zambia extradite them?"

"Who? You can't extradite a tour group. You have to extradite a person. What person do you want to extradite? I have no idea who did it. You have no idea who did it. I'm sure they have no idea who did it."

"Son of a bitch," I said. "What happens when we go back to Zambia?"

"Well, that's the thing. As soon as we're back in Zambia, the Embassy will step in. You'll all be detained, the tour will be shut down, and I'll be ruined. But never mind me. How happy are you going to be missing your flight back to the states?"

"They can hold us?"

"It's a murder. So I need you to step up your investigation. Hell, I need you to *make* an investigation. I can't see that you're doing anything at all."

"We're on the river."

"Not today, we weren't. What did you do today?"

"Watched a cheetah kill an impala."

"Did you talk to anyone?"

"Yeah. One of the librarians. Pam."

"Did you *initiate* the conversation?"

"What's that got to do with it?"

"You didn't, did you? She spoke to you. She spoke to everyone. She's the one making the investigation."

"So why didn't you invite her into your tent? Not dressed for it?"

"It's not funny. We've only got a day and a half on the river. I can stretch it out a day, but that's it. We gotta go back. I need something by then."

"What do you want me to do?"

"The wind's dying down. Tomorrow we'll be back on the river. When we stop for lunch, I'll make the announcement. Tell them about the lab report. Then I'll wander off on some pretext or other. That will get everyone talking. You'll be able to talk to everybody because you'll have a reason. Talk to the librarian particularly. See what she's found out. Take her into your confidence. At least make her think you are. She have any ideas so far?"

"She suspects Jason."

"Interesting."

"Why?"

"Moody, morose loner. Isn't that how the neighbors always describe the killer?"

"You read a lot of fiction?"

"I read the newspapers. So she suspects Jason."

"It's not that she suspects him. She thinks Alice suspected him."

"Oh, she knew that, did she? Interesting."

"What do you mean?"

"Sorry. Vague referent. By she I meant Pam, not Alice. Pam knew Alice suspected Jason."

"Never mind the linguistics. Are you saying you knew Alice suspected Jason too?"

"Of course."

"How did you know?"

"Duke told me."

"How did *he* know?"

"From questioning the guests."

"But Pam didn't tell him."

"He figured it out."

My opinion that it would be a wonder if

Duke ever solved the crime was morphing into a wonder that he hadn't solved it already.

"If you knew Alice suspected Jason —"

"Why didn't I place him under surveillance and take away all sharp objects? Alice was not the authority on the crime. After she's killed, her views take on more weight."

I wandered back to my tent. Nothing ate me. That was the good news.

The bad news was I had to solve a murder and I didn't have a clue.

40

ALARMS IN THE NIGHT

I didn't sleep well. Not surprising after chasing a cheetah, being charged by an elephant, and asked to solve a murder in forty-eight hours or less. But what really kept me up was Malarone and our unflushable toilet.

I needed water.

Yes, I know it was the middle of the night. But our bathroom was small, our tent was small; they occupied basically the same space. I was going to flush that toilet if it killed me. Which, considering the wildlife I was apt to encounter late at night, was entirely likely.

Nonetheless, I hauled my portable sink out to the bush shower, stood it under the shower head, and pulled, hoping more of the resulting water would go in the sink than on me.

It didn't. The shower was dry as a bone. Probably to be expected.

All right. Plan B.

I made my way down to the dining area. The big table was bare. So were the serving tables. The liquor had been put away, probably to keep the staff from getting drunk, or, more likely, the guests.

There was a cooler underneath the table. It held soda and beer. If I was lucky, the ice in it would have melted.

I wasn't lucky. The soda and beer were gone, and the ice had been poured out.

There was a metal pitcher. It sat on the table for the people mixing drinks. It was empty, of course, and it wouldn't have been enough. But it was a pitcher.

Plan C.

I dragged the portable sink down to the bank, filled it by dipping the pitcher in the river. It worked fine. In no time at all the sink was full. Of course it was heavy and hard to carry with water sloshing around. I had to take the pitcher up to the table, come back for the sink. Even then I had trouble. Halfway back to the tent I considered pouring some of the water out. I also considered checking into a hospital, hitching myself up to an Imodium drip, and never taking Malarone again.

It was about then it struck me that I was damn lucky my splashing about hadn't attracted a croc.

I finally got back to the tent. The trick now was to get through to the bathroom without waking Alice.

The tent flap was a problem. It didn't open wide enough to carry the sink straight in. I had to take it sideways. That aimed the light in Alice's direction. I backed out, turned around, took the other side in first. It worked relatively well. Alice said "Mmmph," turned over, and went back to sleep.

I wrestled the sink into the bathroom, dumped the water into the toilet. I could practically hear the Hallelujah Chorus as it flushed.

And I still had half a sink worth.

I was a genius.

Life was good.

I lay down on my cot, switched off the light, basked in my victory.

Until I remembered the pitcher.

I'd left it on the serving table. Nothing wrong with that. Except I'd dipped it in the river. And no one knew it. They'd use it without washing it and poison the camp. I'd be Typhoid Mary. Or Typhoid Dengue. Or Typhoid Malaria. Or Typhoid Typhoid. Or whatever the hell you called whatever the hell you got from drinking river water. I didn't mean Typhoid Malaria. What an idiot. I meant Malaria Mary. And —

I sat up in bed, fumbled for my headlight, switched it on. I slipped my feet into my hiking boots, tied them off loosely without bothering to lace them all the way, and went out.

Walking by one of the tents I heard a little half-moan half-cry. It was quickly stifled. Whose tent was that? I had no idea. But if that was what I thought it was, it must be Simon and Trish. Unless the librarians were lesbians. Or the guys were gay. Or Victoria was into her sister. But, no, it had to be Simon and Trish. Which wasn't fair. Why should they be the married couple having all the fun? The guy didn't even paddle well.

I went back to the table. The pitcher was still sitting there. I should have brought a pen and paper to leave a note. I wasn't going back to get it. I improvised. I took the pitcher, scooped up a little dirt with it, and lay it on the ground with the dirt half-in half-out. They'd have to wash it.

I wondered if they'd wash it in the river.

The tent was quiet on the way back. Clearly, Simon had no staying power. But he had gotten lucky. I wondered if I should wake Alice up, tell her about it. Point out such activity was permissible.

I figured I'd have more luck with the crocodile.

I kicked off my boots, snapped off the light, and got back into bed.

I lay there in the dark and pretended I didn't need to use the toilet.

41
RUDE AWAKENING

I dreamed Clemson was wrestling a crocodile. I was rooting for the crocodile because
I had winners, and I didn't want to wrestle
Clemson. I think first prize was Victoria, or
Annabel, or a threesome with the two of
them. Victoria was rooting for Jason, which
made no sense to me, and Alice was rooting
for me, which did, only if I won she wasn't
going to let me keep the prize because it
would have clashed with the other objects
in her wall unit, which really made no sense
because I wasn't about to hang Victoria on
the wall. And the losers had to dance with
Duke, which I didn't want to do because he
could send them directly to jail. And Keith
walked by making a Trish face just to mock
me for not being allowed to paddle. I
wanted to say something to him, except I
was onstage in a play I'd never rehearsed
and didn't know the lines and I couldn't
wait for intermission because I really had to

go to the bathroom only we were at our second river camp and they didn't have bathrooms, just bedpans kept under the cots.

I woke up to a bloodcurdling scream. I've heard the expression, but I think it was the first time I'd ever heard the scream. If my blood didn't curdle, it must have been the drugs I was taking. I sprang out of bed and nearly collided with Alice, who had just come back from greeting the sunrise.

I hopped into my safari pants and followed her out.

People were emerging from their tents in various stages of undress. Keith was shirtless and proud of it, striking poses for anyone willing to look. No one was. They were all gathering in front of the tent where I'd heard Simon and Trish the night before. Something must have happened to one of them. I saw Simon in the crowd, so it had to be Trish. How could it possibly be Trish? You'd think she'd be immune from anything bad happening for making the Trish face.

She was. I spotted her in the crowd. She was pushing forward, trying to see what was going on.

I pushed past her, tried to reach the tent.

I was prevented by Bono, who blocked my way and said "No, no," just as if he were telling me not to paddle.

I was having none of that. We were on land, not water. I ducked around him to the entrance of the tent, peered in.

One cot was empty.

Clemson knelt next to the other, hunched over the woman in it. He heard me and turned his head. His eyes were wild and crazed. He looked like *he* was making a Trish face.

I saw why.

The woman in the cot was Pam.

Clemson's hunting knife stuck out of her chest.

42
POSTMORTEM

"This is a disaster," Clemson said.

"No one really thinks you did it," I assured him.

"Of course I didn't do it," Clemson said irritably. "I mean it's the end of my business."

"It's also a little hard on Pam."

"How can this have happened?"

Clemson looked as if his whole world had collapsed, which in effect it had. The tour was on hold and most likely canceled. All tour members were confined to their tents, with the exception of Edith, who had a corpse in hers. She had taken a sedative and was asleep on Clemson's cot. A staff man was watching outside.

No one was allowed to leave until the police got there, which they would. The actual police, not just the park ranger. A whole gaggle of officers and detectives along with various big shots from the U.S. Embassy eager to throw their weight around. This time it was the diplomatic trifecta, a murder of an American citizen in Zimbabwe, and the cast of *Mandingo* would be arriving en masse to rain on Clemson's parade.

Clemson and I were seated at the dining table. It had the advantage of being near the coffee urn, which still had some foul dark liquid in it.

"It's not the end of the world," I told him.

"It might as well be. This business is all I have. My wife left me, took the house, the car, and most of the cash. She had a hell of a lawyer. I had to pay him too. Never understood that."

I didn't understand divorce law either.

I was sure Alice did.

"Hey, look. If the police clean this up quickly —"

"Yeah, sure," Clemson said. "It's a triple homicide, only one of which took place in this country. How long do you think it's going to take a government bureaucracy to sort through that?"

"Well, when you put it that way."

"You know what losing my business does to my alimony? Absolutely nothing. I gotta keep paying it."

"How long until they get here?"

"Four or five hours. Depends how long it takes to get their act together. They have to drive down from Harare. Probably start dribbling in around lunch."

"We're having lunch?"

We'd had breakfast, such as it was, before being sent to our tents. Toast, oatmeal, and coffee, most of which had been cooked before we found the body. The bread was toasted over the campfire by Clemson. I half expected him to throw himself in it.

"We'll have lunch. Don't expect much."

"Yeah. So how'd the killer get ahold of your knife?"

"That's the first question the police are going to ask me."

I figured that was probably the *second* question the police were going to ask him. The first was, Did you kill her?

"When's the last time you saw it?"

"I don't know. The last I *remember* seeing it was in the jeep, when I pulled it out to wave in that moron's face."

Clemson speaking derogatorily about a guest was an indication of how upset he must be. On the other hand, it was only Keith. Anyone could be excused for not liking Keith.

"Did you take it out of the sheath?"

"Didn't you see me?"

"I don't mean then. I mean later, when you got back to the tent, took your equipment off."

"I never take it off the belt. Except when I wash the pants. You know how often that is out here?"

"You leave the belt in your pants when you take 'em off?"

"Sure, don't you?"

"Yeah, but I don't have a knife on it. You didn't notice it was missing when your took off your pants?"

"If I had, I'd have known it was gone. I didn't know until I saw it in the body."

"Could someone pull it out of the sheath while you were wearing it?"

"Not unless they wanted their arm broken."

"When could someone take it?"

"While I was in the shower."

"Or while you were asleep?"

He shook his head. "Not a chance. I'd wake up. I'd know someone was there."

I was sure he would. So it could only have been taken while he was in the shower. That left a very narrow window of opportunity.

"That's the situation," Clemson said. "Can you help me?"

I couldn't think of how, but I had to say something. He was in such distress, I couldn't let him down. I could question people in a last-ditch effort to get to the truth before the police got there, not that it would matter. In all likelihood, even if I solved the damn thing the cops wouldn't care. They'd reject the solution just because it was mine. Alice would pooh-pooh it too. Of course, the police didn't know Alice. If I could get to them before she did —

Good lord, there I was, grasping at straws, having flights of fancy and worrying about my problems while Clemson was in abject despair suffering the torments of the damned, desperate for the slimmest words of encouragement, be they hollow, hoping, if only for the briefest of moments, to occupy his mind with something other than his personal and financial ruin. All he wanted was for me to say that I would help him if I could. He hadn't asked for anything specific, he just wanted to know if I could do *anything.*

I couldn't lie to him.

I sighed, shook my head.

"No."

43
MY RIGHT LEG

I lay on my cot, brooding about what was to come. Our safari was over. Of that there was no doubt. Not that we would lose anything. Alice, of course, had trip insurance, and the only thing that had stopped her from filing for it already was the fact we had no Wi-Fi service. She was on the iPad, editing yesterday's pictures and the ones she shot of the sunrise. There were no safari pictures from today. And Alice isn't big on crime-scene photos, not that I blame her, but it would have been nice. It would have given me something to work on. If I had an iPad, of course.

Instead, I lay on my back, waiting to be called.

As predicted, I didn't crack the case before lunch, and the full complement of local law enforcement, national law enforcement, and international law enforcement that arrived had wanted food and conversation. The staff had whipped up hamburgers, which were supposed to have been for dinner, but Clemson was pulling out all the stops in the hope of appeasing the unappeasable, while the police milled about, marking their territory and fighting over jurisdictional rights.

All of this took a lot of time but eventually resulted in a schedule of interviews, all likely to be equally fruitless. By schedule I don't mean *we* had a schedule: the police did, in terms of who got to talk to people first. We, the great unwashed, were chosen at random to submit to this series of interviews, all conducted according to a particular pecking order, strictly adhered to unless one of the interrogators wanted to see someone again.

Thwarting all of their efforts was the ambassador from the U.S. Embassy, hopelessly torn between safeguarding the rights of the suspects and safeguarding the rights of the deceased.

I could see why Clemson doubted their prospects of success.

I hadn't gone yet, which was just as well, as I had nothing to contribute except hearing sounds from the tent, which, were they lethal rather than amorous, would have placed the time of death around midnight, which any medical examiner worth his salt could have done anyway.

I'm not sure the medical examiner they brought along did anything more than pronouncing the body dead, but at least he got it moved out of the tent. It was in a van on its way back to civilization.

I envied it.

I had not spent the morning going tent to tent. I was sorry to let Clemson down, but no one needed that. I'd have been about as popular as the Ebola virus. I hung out in our tent, listened to Alice explain how we were getting our money back. She didn't have to convince me, but she couldn't get through to the travel agent so I was the substitute punching bag.

During lunch, our tour group had huddled away from the cops and discussed insurance claims, alternate travel plans, intentions to wash out undies, requests for Tylenol, and whose toilets worked, which turned out to be no one's. In short, anything but the crime.

After lunch, we'd returned to our tents to await our impending interrogations in our third straight murder investigation. I sat outside to see who they took first. It was Edith, of course, the bunkmate of the deceased. Who they chose next might have been illuminating, but so might staring at a Ouija board. Which was why I was lying on my cot trying to think things out.

Edith was the most likely suspect. She had the opportunity. Moreover, her presence practically precluded any other killer. The tent was small. It would be hard to enter it and stab Pam without waking Edith. Maybe you could get in from the side, slip your arm under the mesh mosquito netting and the rolled-down canvas side flaps, slide the knife up between the cot and the side of the tent, plunge it into Pam and release it, letting your arm slide out. You'd have to rely on a single thrust, accurate and lethal, but it could be done.

But as Sergeant MacAullif, my cop friend from the city, liked to point out, just because a thing was possible didn't mean it happened.

No, Edith was clearly the most likely suspect.

Next would be Clemson. Edith had the opportunity, but Clemson had the means. The murder weapon was his. Someone could have taken it while he was in the shower, but how would the killer have known he would be in the shower? Or was that just coincidence? Was the killer looking for *any* murder weapon that could be identified with someone else? Not likely. When it came to means, Clemson won hands-down.

He flunked out on motive. Clemson had no motive for the crime. Quite the opposite. It ruined his business, ruined his life. Nothing could induce him to do it.

Nothing.

I read too many murder mysteries, but when a person has a perfect anything I suspect him. A perfect alibi. No motive. Warning bells go off. Was that really true, or did it just seem that way?

Clemson had a strong motive *not* to kill Edith.

Could he have had a *stronger* motive to kill her anyway?

And what could that possibly be?

Killing her destroys his business and brings about his financial ruin. What could be worse than that?

Well, how about death? You hear about a fate worse than death, but isn't that hyperbole? Well, maybe not. Maybe stockbrokers really do jump out the window when the market collapses. But say for the sake of argument that Clemson would rather go broke than die. Was Pam a lethal threat? Hard to fathom.

All right. What about incarceration? Clemson was an outdoors man, flourished in the wild. He would do almost anything to stay out of jail. Even give up his business. Going to prison would end his business anyway. Sort of the lesser of two evils. Jail and destitution, or just destitution. Kind of a no-brainer.

Okay, Clemson will do anything to stay out of jail. Why does he kill Pam? She could send him there. How? Obviously, she found something that implicates him in the other killings. Which only follows. If Clemson is the killer, he committed all three. He killed Pam because she figured out he killed Alice. He killed Alice because she figured out he killed Daniel.

So why did he kill Daniel? Well, Daniel trafficked in drugs. Drugs were a threat to his business. He eliminated the threat.

But why kill him? Why not just fire him?

Maybe he couldn't. Maybe Daniel had something on him. It was blackmail, not drugs. Clemson wasn't the type to submit to blackmail. Daniel had to be killed. He had to be killed, and it couldn't look like murder. That's why he went to such elaborate lengths, dragging the body to the sausage-fruit tree, making it look like one fell on his head. How long had it taken Clemson to find a sausage fruit on the ground? Had he had to climb the tree to get one? If I had looked closely at the sausage fruit, would I have noticed that the stem had been sliced in half by Clemson's hunting knife?

I shook my head to clear it.

What was I doing? Succumbing to a storybook plot. Thinking the *least* likely person committed the crime.

I needed to stop my mind. I looked at Alice. She was still busy with the pictures.

I realized that I'd shot some too.

I took out the video camera, rewound the tape, pushed PLAY.

I had some shots of people paddling canoes down the river from the point of view of someone *not* paddling down the river, a few crocodile and hippos, always from a safe distance, and various assorted animals along the bank.

I also had some very shaky shots of people running through the bush in the hope of seeing a lion, and shots of the same people walking for the same reason to no avail. Since they were all shot from behind, they were not particularly memorable. Of course the camera wasn't rolling for the Trish face.

I had half of an elephant charge. Then the camera went in all directions when I fell down. By the time I got it focused again, the elephant was standing there as if nothing had happened.

I had a few shots of cheetah cubs sleeping. A shot of Mommy standing up and starting to move. Then a lot of footage jumping around crazily in and out of focus as the jeep rocketed through the meadow in hot pursuit. Finally Mommy holding the impala by the neck.

According to the timer on the camera, all that footage took a whopping seventeen minutes. I still had a lot of afternoon to fill.

I remembered I had another tape. The buffalo charge I never got to see because the battery was dead. I scrounged through the backpack, dug it out, stuck it in the camera, and hit REWIND. Nothing happened. Of course not. The tape was already rewound. That was how I'd run the battery down.

I hit PLAY, lay back in my bunk to watch the show.

It was weird seeing the beginning of our trip. I had a shot of the airport. Not Lusaka. The landing strip in the bush. I saw the second airplane arrive, disgorging the four women, Victoria and Annabel, and Pam and Edith.

I had a few shots of assorted impala along the road, back when I was wondering if that was all there was. And then the first camp, the one Clemson slipped in for one night to make us think this was a luxury tour. Some shots of elephants in camp, a highlight, and hippos in the river too far to see.

I had shots from the night drive that hadn't come out well, despite all Daniel's efforts with the searchlight. They were hard to see now, knowing he'd been killed. As were shots of Alice and Pam.

Among the poorly lit shots, alas, were the leopard and hyena, the highlight of the night drive.

Despite John tying the record, I hadn't caught a single shot of a genet.

There were shots of the first bush camp. I finally got to see the bull charging. Or rather the bull retreating: I missed the whole charge, but I had a damn good shot of him racing out of sight.

And I had shots of the aftermath, shots I hadn't realized I'd taken. Shots of Alice with her camera, and Victoria and Keith on the ground. I wondered if there was any way to zoom in. I remembered the expression on Victoria's face, but I would have liked to see the one on Keith's. It seemed to me there was a note of malicious triumph, of macho glee. The type of look a movie star's publicist would pay a fortune to keep out of the tabloid press. The type of look that could end a career, at least a career as a leading man. One look at that and Victoria would never give Keith a second thought. Not that she would anyway. Her interest was in Jason.

Was there a shot of him?

He wasn't in the frame. Where had he been standing when the bull charged? More to the point, where had he been standing *after* the bull charged? Had he dived for cover? Not likely. Then he'd have been on the ground too.

The camera didn't look for him. Instead it hung limply at my side and filmed forty-five minutes of my leg.

Well, at least I'd figured out when I left it on.

Actually, the footage of my leg was by far the most interesting. The camera was rolling, but I wasn't pointing at anything, so people weren't inhibited by it. No one was making comments for the sake of my soundtrack. They were just being themselves.

Keith was just being a jerk. Whatever the situation, he did not disappoint. He could always be counted on to say something arrogant, crude, and offensive, sometimes to women, but often to one and all. So the audio portion was pretty damn good.

The video left a bit to be desired. Granted, it was a mighty fine leg, as any impartial observer would be forced to concede; still there was such a thing as too much of a good thing. Nor was it always appropriate. The footage of me marking my territory, for instance, might need to be edited.

I kept waiting for someone to say something relevant, like, "I wish we didn't have to kill Daniel," but nobody did. Anything would help. A nuanced remark. A strained inflection. I hadn't heard one, but I didn't give up hope.

The camera was still rolling when we stopped for sundowners. I recalled that was when I was going to question the guests after the Alice 2 murder. Only Annabel was busy protecting Victoria from Keith so I hadn't done it. Instead I'd made an abortive attempt to talk to Jason, who'd blown me off as quickly as possible without uttering one helpful word.

Of course the minute I had that thought, the whole mystery-story mentality kicked in. One helpful word. My rash assumption that there hadn't been one didn't mean there had, but you could have fooled me. I listened very carefully to the audio portion of the encounter.

Unfortunately, I'd done most of the talking. Our first exchange was my "Pretty exciting, eh?" and his "What?"

The rest of his responses were: "What murder? The woman died in her sleep," "No one gave her poison," and, "I don't know what you're talking about," during the last of which I had a shot of his hand pouring soda out on the ground before walking off to put the can on the table. I recall thinking he'd done it just to get away. While that might have been revealing, it was also effective. I had no more footage of Jason.

I stopped the tape. Rewound. Played it again.

Was there anything there?

"What?" was not particularly helpful.

"What murder? The woman died in her sleep." How did he know that? Was he a doctor? No, he was just denying that it was a murder. Which he'd be eager to do if he was the one who'd committed it.

The same went for "No one gave her poison." The flat denial. Just like any two-bit punk ever picked up for anything: "What wallet? I never took nuthin'."

And finally, "I don't know what you're talking about." The total copout, fleeing the interrogation.

Put that all together and the cops should

be fitting the guy for handcuffs.

Or ignoring, reasonably enough, a particularly innocuous exchange.

I couldn't help thinking there was something I was missing. The first time I'd played the tape, something had registered. It wasn't registering now. Why? Because I was looking for it. I was torturously wrapping my mind around minutiae, looking for subtleties and nuances. Why couldn't I just look at the tape? With no preconceptions. Like the first time.

I rewound the tape. Tried to clear my head. Hard to do. Don't think of an elephant. I smiled. I'd chosen the example at random; but having been charged by an elephant, it was amazingly apt.

And particularly wrong. In this case, I *should* think of an elephant. Anything that cleared my mind from thinking about the conversation.

I hit PLAY. Thought about the elephant. And me slipping on the termite mound. And the camera going every which way.

On the tape Jason was telling me the woman died in her sleep. I barely heard. I was thinking about what Clemson said about ants in my pants. It was enough to make me squirm even now.

And just like that, it was over. Jason said I

336

don't know what you're talking about, dumped out the can of soda, and —

My mouth fell open. It was like being charged by the elephant. I stopped the tape, rewound it just a little, played it again.

There was a PAUSE button. Not STOP, PAUSE. STOP turned the playback off. PAUSE froze the frame.

By the time I found it, Jason was long gone.

I stopped the tape, rewound it again, hit PLAY.

I'd gone back a little further. I got to hear him tell me she died in her sleep. Which gave me time to take my eye off the screen, find the right button, and put my finger on it. I looked back up just as Jason told me he didn't know what I was talking about.

On the screen, he dumped out the Diet Coke.

I froze the frame.

Looked closely.

Frowned.

I looked over at Alice, who was still busy working on her iPad.

"Alice?"

"Yeah?"

"Any way to enlarge this?"

44
CALLING IN A FAVOR.

I went to look for Clemson.

I didn't get far. A uniformed officer stopped me right outside my tent. He gave me what seemed the universal Zimbabwean smile of amazingly white teeth, waggled his finger in my face, and said, "No, no."

"I have to talk to Clemson."

He smiled and nodded, pointed back toward my tent.

Oh, boy. As if things weren't hard enough. I pointed to myself. "I —"

Walked my fingers away. "— go —"

Pointed to my mouth. "— talk —"

Pointed toward the staff tents. "— Clemson."

He looked at me. "I Zimbabwean. Not stupid." At least he didn't roll his eyes. "Why?"

"I have to tell him something."

"About crime?"

"Yes."

"You talk police?"

"I'm going to talk to the police. Right now I need to talk to him."

"Why?"

"He asked me to."

He didn't say anything. He didn't need to. His look said it all. I'd been confined to my tent. We had no phones.

"Before the police got here. He asked for my help."

That sounded ridiculous even as I said it. Miraculously, it worked. He stood aside, let me pass.

I found Clemson sitting alone at the big table.

"How you doing?" I said.

He raised a bleary eye. "I thought you were confined to your tent."

"I'm a smooth talker."

"You talk to the police?"

"They'll probably get to me by tomorrow."

"So you came by to cheer me up?"

"I doubt it. Your business is pretty much finished. Last I heard, people were discussing whether they can sue you for punitive damages on top of cost."

"Good thing you're not here to cheer me up."

"On the other hand, if the police solve this

today, we've still got three days left."

"What are the chances of that?"

"You're probably better off buying a lottery ticket."

"You're here to gloat?"

"No, I'm here to help."

"How?"

"I may have something."

"What is it?"

"It's just a theory."

"What?"

"I should really tell the police."

"Then why are you here?"

"The police aren't going to listen."

"I can't blame them if you talk like this. I'm ready to strangle you."

"That's the problem. You think this is bad? My theory's worse. But I think I'm right, and I think I can prove it. You got any pull with the police?"

"A little. I've helped them with poachers on the river."

"Good. You can collect on the favor. Tonight, before dinner, let's have drinks around the campfire. Invite the police to join us."

"They can't drink on duty."

"That's up to them. They can have soda if they like. But just after dark get the campfire going, give 'em drinks, sit 'em in a circle, let me do my thing."

"What's your thing? What are you going to do?"

"Vote someone off the island."

45
TRIBAL COUNCIL

"Welcome to the tribal council."

I looked around at the circle of angry faces. No one was happy about having spent the afternoon answering a bunch of dumb questions over and over for a bunch of dumb policemen. At least that was their opinion. The relative intelligence of the policemen involved was not to be underestimated. Still, the result of their cumulative interrogation was nil, and I could understand my fellow travelers' displeasure.

No one was happy about delaying dinner either, in spite of the pre-dinner hot showers offered as a subterfuge. Few took them, even if they hadn't in days. No one much cared if they looked like a coal miner or smelled like a skunk. But I needed it dark for the campfire. I had so little to go on, I wanted to use every theatrical ploy in the book.

"I'm sorry to inconvenience you. I know

you'd all like to go to dinner, but first we have this murder to clear up. So, I'm going to tell you who committed the crime, the cops can arrest the perpetrator, we'll be out on the river first thing tomorrow."

Everyone gawked at me as if I'd taken leave of my senses.

If only they knew how right they were.

"We start with Daniel. Daniel was murdered, but we didn't know that at first because the killer went out of his way to make it look like an accident. I apologize for saying 'his.' By that, I don't mean to imply the killer was a man. It's just a pain in the ass to say his or her all the time. If I refer to the killer as he, I mean he or she; if that's sexist I'm sorry, but we'd all like to get to dinner.

"Anyway, whoever killed Daniel made it look like an accident by dragging the body out to the meadow to make it look like a sausage fruit fell on his head. That would tend to indicate the killer was a man, because lugging the body that far might be difficult for a woman. Not impossible, but not likely.

"The murder of Alice Ardsdale is just the opposite. Alice was poisoned, poison is a woman's weapon. Could a man use poison? Of course he could. It's just less likely.

"So, we have a tossup. One crime is most likely a man, the other is most likely a woman. Which possibility is stronger? To put it another way, who is more likely to have done both?

"Then we have the murder of Pam. This one is diabolical. The killer used a knife. Clemson's knife. Does that make him a suspect? Of course. Did he do it? Of course not. It shuts down his business. And you're all talking about taking him to court and hanging his head on your trophy wall.

"To be fair, Clemson might have commited the crime, even though it meant his financial ruin, if he'd committed the first two crimes and Pam had uncovered something that could send him to jail. If you corner an animal he will attack, and no one knows it better. So we can't quite write him off, but we really should."

I raised one finger. "But not the theory. The theory is sound. Pam was killed because she was a threat to the killer. Or because the killer *thought* she was a threat to him. Pam, like Alice, was a mystery buff, and was asking questions about the crime. And the killer was very sensitive. You might even say paranoid. The killer exhibits the sort of schizophrenic personality that would make him think everything was fine one minute and think it was all falling apart the next, that he was about to be discovered, that people were after him.

"That theory works fine for Pam and Alice.

"Daniel is another story. It's hard to imagine Daniel as a threat to anyone. You'd have to be really round the bend. Hallucinating. Suffering not just attacks of paranoia but delusions. No, Daniel as a threat doesn't fly. It had to be something else.

"It was. Daniel had a sideline. Daniel dealt in drugs. And not just marijuana. He dealt in heroin, meth, cocaine. Hard narcotics. The type that could make a person hallucinate. The type that could make a person paranoid. The type that could make an unbalanced person kill."

I paused for dramatic effect. I needn't have. I certainly had everyone's attention. "We are here to vote someone off the island," I proclaimed. I turned in a full circle, looked everyone in the face.

"Jason," I said.

He looked up startled, then lowered his head.

"You're wearing a hat. You always wear a hat, even after dark. Your sunglasses are off, but your hat's down over your eyes. Are you afraid to look me in the face?"

"I don't know what you're talking about," he said.

But he still looked down.

"He knows exactly what I'm talking about. Jason always wears aviator shades, always wears a wide-brimmed hat. After dark he takes off the shades because he doesn't want to call attention to himself, but he hides behind the hat.

"He always wears a safari outfit, long pants, long sleeves. Never short pants, never a short-sleeved shirt. Nothing wrong with that. I do too. Particularly after dark, because of mosquitos. But in the daytime, when it's really hot, I roll the sleeves up. Jason never does.

"Except when he has to wash his hands. Which is usually done in private, back in the tent. Occasionally, out in the bush, Daniel or Phillip or one of the staff will pour water over your hands after you mark your territory or before sundowners. But, aside from that, has anyone ever seen Jason roll up his sleeves?"

I looked around the circle. I was greeted with baffled stares. No one knew what I was talking about. But no one was leaping up to contradict me.

Including Jason.

I turned back to him. "Roll up your sleeves."

He didn't answer me. Made no attempt to do so.

"Come on, Jason, roll 'em up."

"No."

"This is not a game, this is a murder investigation. Roll up your sleeves."

"You can't tell me what to do."

"No, but the police can. They can do pretty much whatever they want. They may not even have to advise you of your rights. I don't know the laws here. If that's the way you want to play it, feel free. One way or another you're rolling up your sleeves."

That, of course, was a bluff. I had no idea if the police could make him roll up his sleeves, or if they'd give a damn if he rolled them up or not. Clemson had called in his favor and got 'em to let me make my pitch, with the argument that I had no official standing so it wouldn't reflect on them if I made a fool of myself, and if I came up with anything it would be a feather in their cap, or whatever Zimbabwean colloquial equivalent they had for such happenstance.

Even so, whether they'd be inclined to go along with this was a somewhat iffy proposition. I just hoped the threat would get a rise out of Jason.

I was not to know.

Unfortunately, the ambassador from the U.S. Embassy chimed in. "Why do you want him to roll up his sleeves?"

Talk about bad timing. I kind of wanted the visual reveal before laying out a rather disjointed and unconvincing explanation. However, you have to work with what you've got.

"Because he has track marks on his arm. That's why he keeps his sleeves rolled down. Because he's a junkie. That's how he got involved with Daniel. He was buying drugs from him. But he didn't bring enough cash to buy all the drugs he wanted. And Daniel wasn't taking checks or advancing credit. When the money stopped, the drugs stopped. But junkies don't stop. Jason killed Daniel to steal his stash.

"Maybe he didn't mean to kill him. He hit him over the head. When he realized what he'd done, he panicked, tried to make it look like an accident. He carried Daniel to the meadow, put him under the sausage-fruit tree. It was easy to do. He was high on drugs with the strength of a superman.

"Ever since, he's been getting high and hiding behind his aviator sunglasses and his safari hat. And striking out at anyone he suspected, in his drug-fueled paranoia, of getting close to uncovering the truth.

"That is why I am asking him to roll up his sleeves, and it will be a lot better if he does it voluntarily than if he insists the police make him do it."

Jason raised his head. I saw his eyes. They were frightened. A cornered animal. He opened his mouth. Closed it again.

"Come on, Jason, roll up your sleeves."

He was about to break. If the ambassador would just shut up. And the police didn't butt in.

They didn't.

Keith did.

He leapt to his feet. "Leave him alone!"

I looked at him. "Why?"

"It's intolerable! Don't you know who this is?"

Jason put up his hand. "Keith!"

"No! It doesn't matter now. This moron is going to get you arrested for having track marks on your arm. Of course he's got track marks on his arm, you idiot! It's no secret he does drugs. Here, look!"

Keith turned on Jason as if he were going to take hold of his arm and forcibly roll up his sleeve.

Instead, he snatched off his safari hat.

Blond hair cascaded down the sides of Jason's face.

There came a startled gasp from the other side of the campfire.

It was Victoria. She was staring at Jason in astonishment. "I knew he looked familiar!"

Keith pointed at her. "That's right," he said. "This is Jason Kleghorn, lead guitarist for Vertical Razor, the latest punk-rock sensation. He's here transitioning out of rehab so he can rejoin the band in time to promote their new album. It debuted at number 4, but should go higher when they preview their new single on Jimmy Fallon, and I'm not going to let him miss it just because you want to make a big deal out of some old needle marks."

The one I judged to be the most senior of the many Zimbabwean police officers stepped into the circle. "Is that true, Mr. Cleghorn?"

Jason looked sheepish. Shrugged. "Yeah."

The policeman turned back to me. I'm not sure if he expected an explanation, an apology, or for me to break down and confess to the crime.

I nearly did. I was dumbfounded at having the rug pulled out from under me. I was utterly dry. For once, I wished the ambassador from the U.S. Embassy would speak up.

He did.

350

The ambassador took a pen and paper out of his briefcase, smiled somewhat sheepishly, and thrust them at Jason. "Excuse me, Mr. Kleghorn. I have a sixteen-year-old daughter. . . ."

46
LICKING WOUNDS

"It's not your fault," Alice said, a supportive statement easily parsed into it *is* your fault, but try not to blame yourself since so many other people are already doing that.

No one had spoken to me at dinner. Not only had I made a complete ass of myself, but I had failed to deliver on my promise to get them on the river in the morning. Instead we were scheduled for an absolutely useless second round of interrogations, this time focusing on who knew Jason was famous and when did they know it.

I had been widely shunned. The only one happy about my big mistake was Victoria, who clearly took the identity of Jason as a vindication of her being smitten, as if his being famous made him automatically a wonderful person, which, I could have told her from experience, was often just the opposite. Still, a young girl's infatuation with a rock star was probably not a unique event in the annals of romance, and yes, I would count Victoria as a young girl in that context; in fact, I would count practically any woman on the south side of senile.

"You made an excellent investigative find," Alice said. "Unfortunately, you jumped to an inaccurate conclusion."

I wondered if I was the only one who would have heard the word "jumped" as a pejorative. "Uh-huh."

"I want to say something."

"What's that."

"You're often wrong."

"Thanks. I needed that."

"I'm serious. What you do is largely guesswork. You're wrong more often than you're right."

"You're really building me up."

"So you expect it."

"I forget. Didn't you open with it's not your fault?"

"So you're not surprised when it happens. You *expect* to be wrong."

"Alice —"

"But that doesn't mean you are."

I frowned. "What are you talking about?"

"Well, look what happened. You laid out a perfectly good case. Then it turns out the guy's famous and can account for the tracks on his arm. Does that make him innocent?

Does that make your whole theory crash to the ground?"

"I don't follow the logic. Do you think he's guilty?"

"That sweet-looking boy? Of course not."

I groaned. "What *do* you think?"

"I think you're too quick to doubt yourself. No, don't argue, you know what I mean. You go from I-solved-it to I'm-totally-lost in a heartbeat. There's never any in between."

"In between?"

"Your theory about the boy was wrong. So you abandon it. A perfectly good theory and you just throw it away."

"Perfectly good?"

"Absolutely. Didn't I say it was damn fine work? You really need to have your hearing tested. You never hear a thing I say."

"I hear everything you say."

"Oh? What did I say?"

I had no idea. My mind was mush. Alice could have told me Clemson was out stalking ant lions and I could have heard it, processed it, and had no idea she said it.

"I'm way too stressed to play games, Alice. What's your point?"

"I told you."

"Tell me again."

"Your idea Jason was buying drugs from

Daniel was excellent. Unfortunately, it was probably wrong. It's entirely likely that Jason *wasn't* buying drugs from Daniel."

"So?"

"Who was?"

47
TRIBAL COUNCIL, TAKE 2

There were audible groans when I stood up.

Everyone had been late for breakfast, not because anyone was dead, but because no one was eager to get up. The staff had to go from tent to tent waking them again and again. When everyone was finally herded into a circle, the first thing they wanted was coffee and toast.

The last thing they wanted was me.

"I know, I know, I'll make it brief. I made a fool of myself last night and you all resent me, and I understand. I had a theory and it turned out it wasn't right. But, as my wife points out, that doesn't necessarily mean it was wrong. Jason has an excuse for having tracks on his arm, he's a rock star. I don't think any of the rest of us are. We have no excuse for having tracks. So let's roll up our sleeves and see who does."

Unexpectedly, nebbishy Simon asserted

himself. "Yeah, well, what if we don't feel like it? Why should we do anything you say?"

"You don't have to, of course. But if you don't, you'll be the first one the police question. And guess what'll be the first thing they're gonna ask?"

His defiance evaporated as quickly as it came. He sank back in his chair.

"So, if we could all roll up our sleeves, hold out our arms."

Everyone did. Some more grudgingly than others, but they all complied. Even Simon. Even Edith. I felt sorry for her having to do it, but I couldn't make an exception. She held out her arms stoically. Her expression was not kind.

Her arms were clean.

So were everyone else's.

With one exception.

One person had not rolled up his sleeves.

"You too, Jason," I said.

He looked surprised. Jason had reverted to his own persona, discarded the hat and shades. His hair hung proud and free. "Why?" he said. "You know I have tracks."

"So you say. But what if you *don't*? What if that's just a cover story to keep up your bad-boy image?"

"Are you kidding me?"

"Yes, I am. That would be utterly whacky

on the one hand, and wouldn't help us at all on the other. I have no doubt you have tracks. But are they fresh? If you ripped off Daniel's stash, you'd have been shooting up ever since. I think we could tell."

"I think you could tell without looking at my arm. If that were the case, I'd have trouble getting out of bed."

"Then you won't mind showing us."

Jason rolled his left sleeve up past the elbow, extended his arm. "Here. Knock yourself out."

I picked up his arm, inspected it. "Pretty impressive. I think you've earned your reputation as a card-carrying addict. Yes, these all look pretty old."

"Of course they are. You think I'd travel with a hypodermic? How dumb is that?"

"Pretty dumb," I said. "Some junkies are. Let's see your right arm."

His smile faded. "Why? I'm not ambidextrous. I can't shoot up with my left hand."

"That's probably true. But this is a murder investigation. You'll forgive us if we don't take your word for it. Come on, roll it up."

Jason rolled up his right sleeve.

I took his arm, looked at it. "You're right. Pretty clean. Except for this."

"What?"

I pointed.

There was a little tiny scab right in the crook of his elbow.

"This right here."

"It's a bug bite. No big deal."

"You don't get bug bites. You never roll up your sleeves."

"Come on, you got long sleeves. You telling me you don't get bug bites?"

"I do, but they don't look like needle marks. You wouldn't mind letting a doctor have a look at that?"

"Oh, for god's sake!" Keith exploded from his chair. "Will you give it up already? It's a bug bite. It's not a needle mark. I mean, what's your theory? He killed the guy, shot up once, and threw the drugs away? How dumb is that?"

I looked him over. "You're pretty upset about it."

"You're damn right I'm upset about it. Your grand theory fell apart, now you're accusing him of murder on the basis of a mosquito bite. I'm responsible for getting him back to LA in time to start the tour. I'm not going to blow it because of the absurd notions of some amateur detective playing cop."

"I'm actually a professional detective," I said. "I get paid for it. I'm not getting paid in this instance, but back in the states that's my job. I do it and I get paid.

"Just like you do. You're getting paid for this vacation, aren't you? You're on the job right now. I knew it, but I wanted to hear you say it. Getting Jason back to LA clean and sober is your responsibility. One you don't take lightly. Witness this outburst. If you blow it, not only do you lose your job, but you never get another one. You get a reputation for not being able to deliver the goods.

"Jason got out of rehab. Your job was to pick him up, take him to Africa, keep him on the straight and narrow till you get back to LA. And what happens? You get to bush camp and run into a drug dealer. Jason escapes your vigilance and manages to hook up. He doesn't have a hypodermic, but Daniel does. Daniel shoots him up. In the right arm, because Jason knows you're monitoring his left.

"Only Jason can't help giving himself away. You're trained to look for such things. The more he tries to act like he's not high, the more you realize he is."

I glanced around confidently, as if I knew what I was talking about. I didn't, of course, I was making it up out of whole cloth. I just hoped my wild theory was close enough to work.

"You sneak out, hook up with Daniel, pretend you want to score. Nail down the fact he is the dealer. Then you read him the riot act. Jason is off limits, he's not to go near him again. Daniel is nodding and smiling and couldn't be more agreeable, and you can tell he doesn't mean a word of it, he's laughing at you. Furious, you grab the stick and hit him over the head.

"You ditch the body and start covering your tracks. You ditch Daniel's stash. So if the police figure out it was murder, they'll think he was killed for his drugs. Which, in a way, he was.

"The police never suspect, but others do. Alice and Pam get on the scent, and you have to kill to cover it up. I don't know where you got the arsenic, it's used in mining, maybe Daniel got ahold of some, I don't know why, but maybe you found it in his stash, and decided to hang on to it. Until you used it, of course. Then it had to go.

"The next weapon of choice was Clemson's knife. He waved it in your face, so it was nice to pay him back. You really do have a cruel streak. But the knife was a nice touch.

"Too bad you left fingerprints on it."

Keith sneered. "There's no fingerprints on the knife."

"How'd you know that?"

"The police told me. In the interrogation."

"No, they were withholding that fact. But you knew it anyway."

His eyes faltered. Just for a second, but it was enough. "No, no," he protested. "I heard it from the cops."

The senior policeman pushed his way into the circle. This time he had two officers with him. On his signal, they stationed themselves on either side of Keith.

"If you would come with us please, I have a few questions."

The policemen took Keith by the arms and led him away.

It all happened so fast, everyone sat there stunned.

I shrugged. "Well, let's have some breakfast and get out on the river."

48
VICTORY DRINK

Clemson couldn't have been happier. Or more grateful. I think he would have given me a full refund, if he hadn't been faced with the prospect of refunding a couple of days' worth to everyone. Considering that, the man was ecstatic.

"I can't believe it," he said. "Five minutes. It took you five minutes to trap him. I've never seen anything like it."

"Second time around," I said. "Which is the basis of my technique. Keep accusing people, eventually you'll be right."

"What I can't understand is the bit about the fingerprints on the knife."

"Oh, that."

"It didn't make any sense. If the police were withholding it, they wouldn't have told you."

"Yeah. Well, no one mentioned any fingerprints, so I figured there weren't any."

"You made it up."

"I had to."

"Because there's no way you could have known."

"You know that and I know that. Keith isn't as quick as you. And he was that type of guy. Impulsive. Street-smart. But not swift. Remember the missing stick?"

Clemson frowned. "What about it?"

"At the time, everyone except me thought Daniel'd been killed by a sausage fruit. I was asking questions, and you came to my tent to tell me to knock it off.

"Keith must have listened in. He followed me to the crime scene, and followed me back to staff camp where I found the murder weapon. That scared the hell out of him. When I went to get you and Duke, he ditched it. Without it, I couldn't prove Daniel's death was a murder.

"But that proved it to me. The minute the stick disappeared, it confirmed my theory."

"Sorry I wouldn't believe you," Clemson said.

"You had good reason not to. But it just goes to show Keith wasn't thinking clearly. If Daniel's death is deemed a murder, the stick showing up behind that tent would be a good indication someone on the staff did it."

"Well, you solved it in spite of me," Clemson said. "I can't thank you enough. Join me in a victory drink?"

"I don't drink."

"That's a shame. A victory cup of coffee then."

He poured a couple. We added milk, clinked cups. Sipped our coffee. Looked out at the river.

"How bad a hit you gonna take on this trip?" I said.

"I don't know. Insurance will cover most of it. My rates will probably go up. My wife will have to wait on her alimony. She's used to that. Her lawyer will have a coronary. But in the long run?" He shrugged. "It's a toss-up. At first people won't want to book a trip where people get killed. On the other hand, they love horror stories. I never tell 'em until the last night, but they always want to hear. The woman who got bit by a croc. The guy who got mauled by a lion. I imagine after a while people will want to go on the one where all the murders happened."

"I suppose."

"Anyway, thanks again," Clemson said. "If there's anything I can do for you. Anything at all."

I considered. "Well, now that you mention it."

"What?"

"I'd kind of like to paddle."

49
COACH

Alice couldn't work her magic on the way home. There were seats for us in economy, and they saw no reason why we shouldn't sit in them.

Alice didn't agree, and the ensuing argument was the stuff of legend. I'm sure Alice would have won had the woman at the ticket counter spoken any English, but her request to talk to her superior had fallen on deaf ears. Either that or the woman was as good as Duke at feigning ignorance. Which is why we sat in coach.

And why I didn't see my teenage dream, Victoria/Lolita on the plane. She and Annabel, who were legitimately in business class, sat alone. Jason was in business class, but he was going to California.

Keith wasn't going anywhere. Zambia and Zimbabwe were already fighting over him, and the United States would probably join the party. He had, after all, killed two

American citizens, albeit one in Zambia and one in Zimbabwe. I don't know who that gave jurisdiction, but luckily I didn't have to figure it out.

The rest of the trip had been good. My boast had been a little cocky — we actually didn't get on the river until after lunch — but no one complained.

And Clemson made good on his offer. I finally got to paddle. Not Alice, thank goodness. That would have been unpleasant for all concerned. I got to paddle Trish. Simon went with Bono. He didn't feel emasculated, he was happy to let me. He must have felt relieved.

I was able to keep up, so Bono was happy too.

We saw lions from more discreet distances, with cubs that actually played instead of slept.

And not one person got killed. I hate to be flippant about that. I felt sorry for Alice 2. And the librarians, both the live and the dead. Pam left behind a husband. And Edith lost a friend. Even if they only met online, they were good together. I wondered if Edith would post about it on Dorothyl. Or if they only discussed fiction, not true crime. She'd have to be tactful. Pam subscribed to Dorothyl. Her husband would still get the e-mails. Not that he'd necessarily read them. Even if he didn't, could Edith bear to do it? Or would she feel she was trivializing the death of her friend?

Anyway, she rallied, finished the trip, didn't cut it short and go home. I think she genuinely enjoyed the lion cubs. Everyone loves cubs.

So, in spite of everything, the trip ended on a positive note.

Except for the flight. Having tasted business class, economy didn't sit well with Alice. I was reminded of the song that goes, after you've been eating steak for a while, beans, beans taste fine. I didn't quote it to Alice. She would not have been amused.

To Alice, economy was a personal affront. She was not happy, and she didn't care who knew it. Including and especially me.

I could have done without a cranky wife, but aside from that, I was perfectly happy with economy.

As far as I was concerned, it was luxury.

It had a working toilet.

ABOUT THE AUTHOR

Parnell Hall is an Edgar, Shamus, and Lefty nominee, and is the author of the Puzzle Lady crossword puzzle mystery series and the Steve Winslow courtroom dramas. An actor, screenwriter, and former private investigator, Hall lives in New York City.

The employees of Thorndike Press hope you have enjoyed this Large Print book. All our Thorndike, Wheeler, and Kennebec Large Print titles are designed for easy reading, and all our books are made to last. Other Thorndike Press Large Print books are available at your library, through selected bookstores, or directly from us.

For information about titles, please call:
   (800) 223-1244

or visit our Web site at:
   http://gale.cengage.com/thorndike

To share your comments, please write:
   Publisher
   Thorndike Press
   10 Water St., Suite 310
   Waterville, ME 04901